# Table of Contents

I0676808

# Cut down to size

## A Sebastian Cork Novel


By Neal Davies

Sebastian Cork

A copy of this publication can be found in the National Library of Australia


ISBN 9780980874877 (paperback)
ISBN 9780994570505 (ebook)

Publisher Cathie (Catherine) Anne Davies

Six forty-five in the morning, the third Sunday of Spring and the powder blue sky is chilly but crystal clear. Sebastian wakes with baggy eyes, muffles a yawn then quietly dons his casual clothes. He would normally enjoy a sleep in but today is different. Since walking away from his practice as a noted psychologist and lecturer, he has been hired as a consultant for the police and has come to realise how unfit he is; so he is resolved to take as many long strolls as he possibly can, whenever he can.

After Sebastian brushes his thick salt and pepper hair, he goes back into the bedroom to take a lengthy admiring look at his wife Cynthia's delicate face and as she remains fast asleep between their silk sheets, he kisses her on the forehead. Then he paces downstairs dressed in navy cargo pants, polo shirt and sneakers.

On the landing, he pauses for a moment to scan his reflection in the hallstand mirror. It draws furrows on his brow and he scowls at his slightly overweight physique. "It's about time you got off your fat end and did something, old man!"

His disappointed mood soon dissipates as Sebastian takes his first step outside. The early morning air is crisp and has a bite to it. Sebastian's eyes light up and a childlike smile veils his face. The cold freshness smells of lavender and jasmine and the night's dew shines its silver specks across the vivid green carpet of lawn. Happy memories of Sebastian's childhood overwhelm his senses within a moment, as he takes a deep breath and exhales forcefully; producing a misty haze just like it did in the days when innocence ruled his world.

He gazes reflectively, wondering why it has taken him so long to get motivated to lose the weight he has been carrying for a few years and can't believe how good he feels as he scans the surrounding gardens, enchanted by the beauty of the frost on the shrubs and the opalescent spider webs that adorn them like Christmas decorations.

Sebastian sets off at a good pace through the black wrought iron gates that swing sturdily off the creeper-covered, white concrete walls. They are rarely closed and so there is no break in his gait as he pushes up the road toward the lake, like a man possessed.

He is overtaken by the odd jogger along the way and he finds himself stepping up his pace each time only to ease off when he feels his legs burn and quiver. A quarter of the way through his walk his mobile phone begins to vibrate and, in the cold, his fingers fumble to retrieve it from his pocket. It's Paul Lyon, the young detective who's been assigned by Chief of Police Jim Johnson to partner Sebastian during investigations.

"Hi, Seb. It's Paul. Sorry to bother you on a Sunday but Jim called and wants us to attend a murder scene ASAP. He said this one looks like it might be something you'd be interested in. Apparently a jogger discovered a body in Truscan Park at six o'clock this morning."

Sebastian's a little disconcerted as he was thoroughly enjoying his first real attempt at exercise. "What makes him think this particular case will interest me?" he replies with concealed enthusiasm.

"I'm not sure, Seb. I haven't been to the park myself. That's why I rang; I thought you might want a lift."Despite the interruption to his morning stroll, there is nothing in Sebastian's world that can override his enthusiasm for a new case, so he turns and heads toward home. "Thanks, Paul, I appreciate that. It will take me about thirty minutes to get back and another fifteen to have a shower, so if you can pick me up in about an hour that will give me time to have some breakfast as well."

"No problems, Seb. I'll see you then."

By the time he gets back, Cynthia is up and about and looks at him curiously as he walks through the door. "I thought you'd be gone longer, otherwise, I would have had breakfast waiting for you."

Sebastian is still a little out of breath after stepping up his pace on the trip home in order to salvage something from his morning exercise; so he takes a short moment to compose himself. "Yes, I thought I would be too but it seems that murderers enjoy inconveniencing people at inappropriate moments. I'm going to take a quick shower, my love, but if you're still interested in making me the breakfast you just spoke of, I'll be back down in approximately fifteen minutes."

Before Cynthia has a chance to reply, Sebastian is halfway up the stairs, leaving her in reflective silence, wondering what murderer he's talking about and whether he will be leaving sooner or later. Hands on her hips, she sighs heavily as her eyes follow him upwards. She can't help herself from exaggerating her true inner feelings and it doesn't take long for her deepest thoughts to work their way to the surface. "All these years and I don't think I'll ever understand why he does what he does!"

She smiles with an abstract contentment, turns elegantly on her heels and glides toward the kitchen. Sebastian spends a bit longer upstairs than his self-allocated fifteen minutes and Paul arrives earlier than expected. Dressed and famished after his morning stroll, Sebastian rapidly flows down the stairs and once in the foyer, he inhales the sweet aroma of coffee and freshly cooked pancakes topped with maple syrup that float alluringly through the air, adding to his craving. His mind races with joy when thinking about the hardy breakfast awaiting him in the next room but as he enters the kitchen he finds Paul nestling back in **his** chair eating **his** pancakes and drinking **his** coffee.

Paul his mouth half full smiles up at him. "Wow, Seb! You never told me how beautiful your wife is and not only that, she's a great cook as well!"

Cynthia standing by the stove watching Paul devour his meal is flattered by his comment. She tilts her head slightly to one side and smiles affectionately at him and then rapidly swings her attention toward her husband with a piercing glare. "Sebastian Cork! Paul's nothing like you described him. He's a lovely young man."

The smile magically reappears on her face as she looks back toward their guest. "Would you like some more, Paul? I have to put some on for Sebastian anyway."

A wad of pancake pushes out his right cheek. "That would be lovely, Mrs Cork."

Sebastian sulkily glares at Paul then at Cynthia who has already started cooking the next batch. "I thought you would have had mine ready by now!" he says with childlike frustration.

Cynthia, nonchalant, looks over her shoulder. "Your breakfast was ready ages ago but, because you took so long in the shower, I could see it going cold and then Paul arrived, so I gave it to him. Paul filled me in about the murder. It's nice when someone presents you with all the details of what's going on!"

Sebastian glares at Paul again and then back at Cynthia like a little boy who's been naughty. "I was going to fill you in over breakfast," he grumbles.

"Oh well, you don't have to bother now,"she replies in a disinterested manner.

Sebastian feeling uncomfortable and slightly outcast tries to regain some ground. "You're in my seat, Paul!" he mutters irritably and Cynthia swings her head around angrily as Paul begins to rise.

"Don't you dare move, Paul! **Sebastian Cork**! Where are your manners? Paul's a guest here and you can use the other chair. They all match, you know!"

Paul looks at Cynthia as if butter wouldn't melt in his mouth. "It's okay, Mrs Cork. As you said, they're all the same, so I'm happy to move."

Paul picks up his plate and coffee and shifts to another chair and there's no doubting the message in Cynthia's eyes. "My **goodness,** Sebastian Cork! If only you had half the manners this young man's got, I'd be grateful."

Sebastian's lips tighten and there is an awkward silence as he plonks himself down in his favourite chair and sits stiffly. Throughout breakfast, he barely utters a word but his eyes take everything in. His wife, on the other, hand is extremely chatty and dotes over Paul like a long lost son. When the two men are ready to leave, she hands Paul a brown paper bag with some pancakes in it. "This should tide you over until lunch," she says sweetly.

"Thanks, Mrs Cork. I appreciate that."

Her grin turns to a beaming smile. "You're welcome and please call me Cynthia."For the first time since breakfast, Sebastian manages a smile as he gazes at his wife in anticipation. "Did you pack me some too?" he says hopefully.

Instantly her smile turns to a frown. "Of course not Sebastian. If you're serious about losing weight, you should know better than to ask for more!" She leans forward to kiss him goodbye. "Ow!" she says out loud as she grabs her chest.

"Are you alright, my love?" Sebastian says with concern.

"Stop fussing, Sebastian, I'm fine. We did a lot of heavy lifting yesterday for the charity ball and I think I may have strained myself," she scowls.

Paul steps out from behind Sebastian. "Are you sure you're alright, Cynthia?"

"Of course, Paul, and aren't you a gentleman for caring! Thank you."

Sebastian turns up the corner of his mouth, "Great! He's a gentleman for asking and I am some sort of over-fussing fool!"Sebastian sways his head from side to side like a wounded bear, grabs his jacket and cane from the hallstand and heads out the door toward the car without a word and Paul in his wake.

Sebastian buckles himself in and casually sits back as he would at home alone in his lounge chair.

The morning air is now dense with exhaust fumes and mist as they scud along toward the city. Paul threads his way through the never ending stream of traffic and wonders why Sebastian hasn't spoken to him since leaving. "Penny for your thoughts, Seb," he says as he gives him a quick glance with concerned eyes.

Sebastian rapidly rotates his head, gives Paul a daggered glare, then abruptly turns his frustrated attention away and steadfastly watches the quick succession of cars and buildings hurtling past his side window. He wants to say what he is really thinking but overcomes his impulse to do so. He realises this isn't the time or the place to air his feelings and yet his reply comes in a hard, calculating manner:

"Just enjoying the scenery and you'd do well to keep your eyes and thoughts on the road ahead."

Paul gives an uncomfortable rapid glance toward Sebastian without finding its mark and naively replies "Oh. Okay."

Sebastian is content to see all the tall grey terrace houses fly past as he knows they will soon arrive at the park and he can concentrate on the job at hand, rather than be caught up in the uncomfortable small talk. But as Paul negotiates a sharp turn to his right the unthinkable happens: two red taillights in front of them close rapidly like a well-oiled vice. Paul's lightning reflexes are up to the challenge and he hits the brakes hard and fast, bringing their car to a screeching halt, a feather's kiss from the red Mustang in front of them.

"Shit! That's all we need, a bloody traffic jam!" he exclaims as the adrenalin continues pumping through his body like an express train. Sebastian has been flung forward which brought a sudden jolt from his seatbelt. With both hands on the passenger dash, he rips his body sideways with eyes that resemble an agitated bull. "Where the hell's your head, man?" he snaps shocked and angry. "You could have killed us both!"

Paul still staring forward throws himself back into his seat and slams his hands on the steering wheel. "How the hell was I supposed to know the jackass in front of me was going to slam his brakes on?"

Sebastian, still hunched forward, takes a deep breath and forcibly exhales through his nose as he glares at Paul from the corner of his eye. "It seems to me you may have been a little close to the car in front or you wouldn't have had to hit the bloody brakes so bloody violently!"

Paul swings his shoulders around and cocks his head back like a gun about to fire an angry bullet. "Look Seb, if I hadn't been far enough back you'd be sitting in the front seat of that Mustang ahead of us and unable to complain due to swallowing your own airbag. Now, that may not have been good for you but it would be a bloody godsend for me! What the hell is eating you anyway? You've been offish all morning."

Sebastian rigidly pushes back into his seat, turns away rapidly and glares out the side window for an uncomfortable moment and then abruptly swings his shoulders back toward Paul and stares through him as if there is something more interesting taking place outside the driver's window. He's determined not to let Paul know how he feels but something inside keeps pushing his attitude to the surface until he can't hold it in any longer.

"**You!** That's what's bloody wrong, **you!** You come into **my** house, sit in **my** chair, eat **my** pancakes and engage **my** wife in conversation to a point where she's disinterested in anything I have to say!"

Feeling exceptionally foolish after his outburst, Sebastian's cheeks become heated, so he returns to gazing intently out of the passenger side window but finds himself shifting uneasily in his seat. Sebastian's mind now racing, agonises over allowing his emotions to override his logical thought and doesn't know how he will conceal an ever-growing sense of guilt.

Paul has shown a degree of poise to this point but enough is enough and with taut lips he sarcastically retorts "Imagine **that**! The great Sebastian Cork unable to contain his emotions... **unheard of**! So there really is a human under the guise of **Mister-I-Never-Lose-Self-Control-Around-Anyone**?"

With nowhere to go, Sebastian feels even more uncomfortable when Paul momentarily takes his eyes off the now steady stream of traffic ahead of them and chastises him further.

"You're kidding me, **right**? You're jealous, **right**? I don't believe it. I drive over to pick you up, I treat your wife with respect and **you're** jealous!"

Sebastian doesn't answer. He knows Paul's right and just how ridiculous he's been. So he continues to stare out in silence and Paul focuses back on driving.

Sebastian has found himself in unfamiliar territory and casts an anxious glance toward Paul as he reflects ruefully on his poor behaviour. He allows some warmth to creep into his voice "As much as this pains me, I have to admit that was a handy bit of driving earlier." Paul hesitantly looks over at Sebastian and a glimpse of an acknowledging smile passes over his lips as he nods his acceptance. Paul's little grin hasn't gone unnoticed by Sebastian's ever watchful eyes, so his face regains its normal seriousness and he gives Paul a staunch look. "Now would you mind getting your eyes back on the road? Or the next time it might not be a near miss!"

As the car reaches the crest of a gently undulating hill atop Truscan Park, they can see a hive of activity down near the gates. A mob of onlookers point and peer noisily, trying to deduce why the police have cordoned off a section of their park.

Paul kills the motor and they approach two officers standing guard by the large sandstone walls. He flashes his badge and they point him toward a hive of police activity which is now slowly winding down. The serenity of the park seems like an unimaginable place for a murder with its plush lawns and tall broad oaks that, over the summer months, give shade to young couples on their blankets. As it is spring, the birds are in full voice and the sound of their mating calls echo through crisp but warming air.

Sebastian ambles his way toward the murder scene and he is deep in thought. This is only his second case and he remains withdrawn silent and with worried eyes; on the other hand, Paul has a liveliness to his step and a determined look on his face.

The police officers' voices grow louder, breaking the serenity of their surroundings as they ready themselves to leave the crime scene. As their numbers thin, Sebastian and Paul, though still a distance away, see in their midst a young man's body seated upright beneath one of the beautiful old oaks. He wears a navy blue tracksuit and, from where they are, the morning dew sits like tiny teardrops on his thinning fair hair and his pale complexion forms an eerie veil over a once warm face

Packed up, the forensic team move toward them; Cameron Buckley, the Coroner, spots Sebastian and keenly heads for him. "How are you, Seb? I think you may enjoy the challenges of this case."

Sebastian greets him with serious eyes and tight-lipped smile, "Really? Why so? You're the second person who's said that this morning."

Cameron turns and waves his head in the direction of the corpse. "Come and I'll show you."

On arrival, Sebastian can see the uniqueness of this case and is immediately consumed with curiosity. The victim's eyelids have been glued open and his mouth is contorted and agape, as though he had suffered extreme agony before his passing. As Sebastian gets even closer his eyes ignite when he sees the victim's legs have been neatly severed below the knees and directly in front of the corpse the missing limbs are propped into an upright position by two small forked branches that have been cut from a nearby sapling.

Sebastian's initial apprehensions regarding the case are clearly defused by his passion for a new challenge, "I see what you're saying, Cameron. This does look interesting. Have you found any identification on the victim?" he asks inquisitively.

Cameron bites his bottom lip and then replies, "No I'm afraid not. We've been through the victim's pockets and found nothing. What we do know, though, is he was killed elsewhere and brought here. His legs were amputated below the knees making the probable cause of death exsanguination. In layman terms, he bled to death when the femoral arteries were cut during the amputation of his legs and as you can see, there is no pool of blood or spatter around or near the victim, so the murder had to be committed elsewhere. Until I get him back to the lab I can only roughly approximate the time of death by the body temperature and rigor mortis and I would most likely put the time of death between six and ten last night. It's not hard to tell from the agonised look on this poor fellow's face... he died slowly and painfully. If the killer had cut from the underside of the legs, the artery would have been severed sooner and his death would be quick and less agonising."

"The inward folding of the upper skin tells us the limbs were severed from the top of the shin and, if you look here," Cameron squats and points to a specific spot on the shin bone, "there are slight deviations where the cut on the bone shows that whoever did this stopped cutting before reaching the artery to prolong this poor young man's suffering. I can't imagine what excruciating pain this unfortunate fellow experienced! One other thing that may be of interest to you; the killer stripped the victim naked before the legs were severed."

Sebastian listens with enthralled interest and an appraising second glance at the body helps him understand what Cameron has concluded. "Ah, yes! I see what you mean," he replies with evident satisfaction.

Paul stands there curious, his head aslant. "Why?" he enquires as he looks askance from one to the other. Sebastian points at the body. "Look at the legs, Paul. They're naked apart from the socks and shoes. The pants still remain unscathed on the torso."

Paul scratches his head. "But couldn't the killer have just rolled his pants up and then cut his legs off?"Sebastian glances at Cameron who lifts his brow. "As you heard from Cameron a moment ago, there's no blood spatter. It would be all over his clothes, his shoes. Where's the smell of death?"

Paul's expression alters as he realises his question has been thoughtlessly put but, before he can rectify his naivety, Sebastian bends down next to Cameron and sniffs the body. "Come here, Paul. Come and smell." Paul and Cameron look peculiarly at each other and then back at Sebastian. "Paul, please come here! I need to know if you have any thoughts on this aroma."

Paul's face takes on a should-I-shouldn't-I look as he hesitantly bends and inhales apprehensively. "What is that?"

Sebastian, with an intent look on his face, takes another sniff. "I'm not sure, Paul, but it is familiar and we need to find out. Anyway, the point is the body has been cleaned of any odour of death."

Cameron smiles at Paul and says, "Listen to him, young fellow. Sebastian Cork has an incredible mind."

Paul, feeling inadequate, doesn't answer, just raises his cheeks and wryly grins briefly. Cameron looks down at the victim in sympathy and says, "Poor beggar! Anyway, I really have to get back, Seb. Good luck with this one."

Sebastian is quick to put his hand on Cameron's shoulder. "Before you go, Cameron?"

Cameron looks earnestly at him. "What is it, Seb?"

"I trust the stomach contents will be checked for a sedative of some sort?"

Cameron grunts his assent, "Yes of course but I have to go Seb or nothing will get done."

As Cameron works his way back, Paul stands at the psychologist's side, staring at the corpse. "What are your thoughts, Seb?"

Sebastian, still squatting and still absorbed, cups his hands over the top of his cane to maintain balance. He regards Paul as if he's an object rather than an animated life form, as he always does when his mind is otherwise occupied. "If you're talking about the young man's identity, this fellow is either a marathon runner due to his shapely but lean calf muscles... or a tri-athlete. My bet would be a tri-athlete due to the muscular upper body and shoulder structure... indicative of a swimmer."

Paul's inquiring blue eyes squint down at him. "How would you know that? That seems to be to be a bit out of a psychologist's scope, don't you think?"

Sebastian looks back at the corpse and continues to scan over it while responding to Paul's remark. "That's an interesting comment, Paul! So because you were in the Special Forces and the Police Force, you only know about shooting guns and arresting people? You don't know how to cook, shop, or play sport?"

Paul's cheeks glow red but before he gets a chance to retract his comment, Sebastian continues. "Some years back I was fortunate enough to be asked by our Olympic Committee to spend some time with a group of athletes who were having trouble overcoming their nervousness before major events. In my spare time, I would often sit and chat to trainers, coaches, physios and doctors." He turns his head to the side and pauses to reminisce then continues, "Yes, it was a truly memorable experience. Anyway let's get back to my thoughts on this!" he insists with more than a reasonable amount of determination.

Before Sebastian can continue, Paul's face fills with excitement and he reaches down and grasps his shoulder. "You're kidding me, right? You actually worked with some of our Olympians. Which ones?"

Sebastian turns his head sharply toward Paul, eyes blazing haughtily. "Why would I kid about that? And you should know I'm not allowed to disclose names of those I work with. I'd be breaking confidentiality! Now, can we get back to the case at hand?"

Paul removes his hand from Sebastian's shoulder and raises his eyebrows and chin abruptly as he gazes over the tree line toward the park's entrance. "Sure, sure. Whatever!"

Sebastian refocuses on the victim. "As I was saying, this poor fellow looks to be a tri-athlete and was probably right up there amongst the best. The sponsorship logos on his top aren't the same as those you'll find on your average run of the mill tracksuit. Find the sponsors and you'll find his identity."

Paul pulls out a pen and notebook and begins jotting down the sponsors' names as Sebastian stands and looks at the victim's nape, then over to the propped up legs. "As for the murderer, he or she will strike again. There is no doubt the legs have significant meaning to the killer."

Paul stops writing. "Is it possible we're looking for a short person?"

"It's possible, Paul, but most people would be short compared to this fellow. Looking at his legs and torso I would estimate he would easily be taller than six feet, seven inches. So it may not be that the killer was short but had an issue with taller men. And when the killer glued the eyelids of the victim open, I feel it was to make a very personal statement such as 'What good are your legs to you now?' or 'So you thought you were above me!'"

"The victim would have had to be sedated to be overpowered unless there was more than one person involved, but I'm of the strong belief that this killing is very personal and I think the coroner will find some type of sedative in the victim's system."

"Cameron said that this young man would have been conscious throughout the ordeal and if you look closely, you can see the marks where he'd been bound. I would say by the width and smoothness of the imprints, the bindings were possibly leather straps and they held fast his neck, wrists and ankles. So once the sedative had worn off, this poor fellow would have awoken and found he was sitting upright on some sort of bench with a vertical board supporting his back. The leather strap that was secured around his neck would have been loose enough to ensure he could see his own legs being severed but if he tried to pull his head back, there would have been either a spike or nail preventing him doing so."

Sebastian tilts the victim's head forward and gently parts the hair on the back of his head. "If you take a closer look you'll see a hole where he's pushed back in agony, only to create further pain." Paul places his hand on the tree the victim is leaning against and bends his head around to get a closer look while Sebastian continues. "Cameron said he was conscious during the ordeal, so I would have to be a fool not to believe that this murder took place in a building that has been soundproofed or in an isolated area well away from other occupied houses."

"You mentioned, when you rang me earlier, that a jogger found the body at six o'clock this morning and Cameron suggested the murder would have occurred approximately between six and ten o'clock last night. Now, let's assume it would have taken a maximum of an hour to clean up the body, place it in a van and bring it here to the park. Then it may take another thirty to forty minutes to cut the props for the legs and arrange the body into position. So we can assume the killer left the scene of the crime around eleven last night and, subtracting the preparation time, he or she would have taken around six hours and twenty minutes to arrive here at the park."

Paul interrupts, "So we need to look at the map and work out what isolated areas there are within a six and half hour radius of the park."

Sebastian, now upright and ready to leave, replies, "Exactly. As for the perpetrator of this crime, we're looking for someone who is of small to average height, a perfectionist who dresses neatly without being a standout. This person is driven by an intolerable hunger to be seen as a godlike figure whom the victims should be answerable to as a judge, jury and executioner if you like, but he or she can also come across as quite average while still being able to conceal their past and evil, narcissistic traits. I also believe this person will kill again if they haven't already done so."

Paul's forehead ripples with a frown. "Are you saying that this could be a serial killer, Seb?"

"I'm not making a statement, only an observation; since I have taken on this new position as a consultant to the police, I have been spending a lot of time researching murderers and serial killers in order to give such qualified opinions. Come on, let's head back to the car and I will explain on the way back."

Back at the car, Paul settles in behind the wheel and starts the motor. "Okay, you've got me intrigued. Tell me your thoughts, Seb."

Sebastian nestles back into his seat and pushes his chin upward, then shrugs his left shoulder so it almost meets his left ear and then does the same with the right side. "I always get a little stiff in the neck on a cold morning, don't you, Paul?"

With a squeal of the tyres, Paul pulls the car out into the heavy traffic and retorts, "No, Sebastian, I don't! Perhaps it comes from old age. Now is there any chance of giving me an explanation as to why you feel this could be a serial killer?"

Sebastian ceases rubbing the back of his neck frowns and glares at Paul from the corner of his eye. "Fine, I will explain. Recent studies show that most serial killers are motivated out of fear of rejection and abandonment or of feeling less than others. They strive for perfection. When this killer took our victim, he or she deliberately and callously prolonged his agony to gain a sense of power over him. Once our friend in the park finally passed, the killer felt that he had helped redeem our victim of his wrongdoings. That's why the eyelids have been glued open; it's a lesson to the victim that he can no longer stand over or look down upon the killer."

Intrigued with Sebastian's summary, Paul remains deep in thought for the rest of the trip back to Sebastian's house.

Sebastian thanks his colleague and is about to get out of the car but abruptly sinks back into the seat. "Of course!"

"What? What's the matter, Seb?"

"That aroma, the one we could smell on the victim's clothes. I knew I'd smelled it before. It was back in the seventies and all the rage; it's called patchouli oil."

Paul looks at him blankly. "Never heard of it."

Sebastian smiles, alights and bids Paul farewell as he closes the car door and strolls up the pathway and through the front door. After resting his cane and hanging his jacket on the hallstand, Sebastian heads into the kitchen where an array of aromas permeates the air. Cynthia is at the stove cooking up a storm, so he walks up behind her and kisses her on the cheek. "Bit early for dinner, don't you think?"

She turns and smiles, "I thought I would get it out of the way as I was hoping to get some work done in the office this evening."

Sebastian pours himself a coffee from the percolator and holds the pot up to her. "Would you like one?"

Cynthia stirring a pot glances back over her shoulder "No, I'm good, thanks. How did your morning go?"

He lounges back in his kitchen chair and sugars his coffee. "It looks to be an interesting case. Quite brutal, actually: legs severed from the corpse, eyelids glued so the eyes could see what was happening below. Yes, quite brutal!"

Cynthia stops stirring and worriedly turns to face him. "How are you coping with that? I mean, honestly, Seb, this is only your second case and the first real corpse you've seen. Are you okay?"

He takes a sip. "Seriously, my love, I'm fine. I've seen a lot worse. Remember when you were a prosecutor and used to bring home photos of the victims?"

"Yes I do, Seb, but seeing a corpse in a photo is a lot different to seeing them at a crime scene!"

Sebastian raises the warm brew to his lips again, takes a swallow and gently places the mug on the table. He rises to his feet and motions for Cynthia to join him and then draws her close. "Trust me, my love, I'm okay. In fact, I am actually looking forward to this case and I promise you, if it ever gets too much for me, you'll be the first to know. Now I'm heading upstairs to change but I need to know that you are okay with what I do."

Cynthia forces a smile and gently nods in the affirmative. He kisses her on the forehead and goes upstairs. When Sebastian returns he finds Cynthia on the phone to her girlfriend, so he makes himself a tuna fish sandwich for lunch and heads into the study to read further on the mindset of serial killers. He becomes so enthralled with his research; time gets away from him until Cynthia comes to get him for dinner.

Now he draws a wage from the police department, Sebastian feels obliged to keep Captain, Jim Johnson, up to date on his progress and will work the rest of the evening on his report. Cynthia has plans for the evening as well and retires to her office to go over some ideas she has for a charitable function and other bookwork. So after dinner, Sebastian pours himself a drink and heads to his office at the rear of the house. Even with both offices at the rear end of their large house, it's not a simple task to move from one to the other quickly. If Sebastian wants to talk to Cynthia he has to walk up the hallway, through the foyer, into the kitchen and down another small hallway to get to her. This was Cynthia's innovation; Sebastian used to barge into her office whenever he felt the need or had lost something and required her help to locate it. Cynthia believed most these interruptions were unnecessary and that much of his reliance was habitual, so she decided to have renovations done specifically to prevent Sebastian's intrusions. It had become a constant distraction for her when they had adjoining rooms and the new design has proven beneficial to him as well, as he now has to rely on his own intuition to find solutions to whatever poses him a problem.

He flicks one of three switches to the left of the doorway and two brass gooseneck lights on the timber-panelled wall gently illuminate his mahogany and oak roll top desk which in turn nestles comfortably on a large red Persian rug. Sebastian always feels relaxed in this room and he parks himself in his matching mahogany swivel chair with satisfaction; the comfort of the green leather cushion can't be matched by any other in the house.

Using his elbows as a prop, Sebastian rests his head by placing his thumbs under each cheekbone and gently massages his forehead with his fingertips. It's been a long day and if he remains in this position much longer there's a chance that he may drift off and not complete the task ahead, so he shakes himself vigorously and pulls a pen and note pad from the drawer. Sebastian is 'Old School' in many ways and will write his thoughts with a fountain pen before typing them.

It is late by the time his thoughts and observations are typed up and printed off. Just as he places them in a cream manila folder, Cynthia, with what Sebastian sees as her psychic mannerisms, pokes her head into his office, smiles lovingly and says, "There's a nice hot cup of cocoa waiting in the kitchen for you if you'd like to join me."

He slumps back in his chair, yawns, then swivels himself around. "Your timing is impeccable, my love. I was just finishing up here."

Sebastian seems to be feeling more aches and pains of late; slowly he rises to his feet and begins to follow her out of the room but before he reaches the door a voice sounds from the hallway. "Don't forget to bring your folder out with you; otherwise, you're sure to forget it in the morning."

Sebastian's eyes float upward. "I already have it with me, darling." He races back to the desk and grabs it. After a brief chat over a hot cocoa, they head upstairs to bed where Sebastian pops the folder on the dresser, and spends a weary night tossing, turning and going over things in his head.

The following morning Cynthia is up before Sebastian and knows her husband detests being late to anything so, she gently shakes his shoulder. "Seb, it's time to get up."

Half asleep, half awake, he grunts. "Oh, really? Is it that time already?"

She can see how tired he is and she tilts her head lovingly. "Yes, my darling, I'm afraid it is. Are you sure you're awake? I need to have my shower now."

Sebastian blinks hard in an attempt to shunt himself into an awakened state. It's not too long before he has all his aching joints moving, so he briskly throws on his dressing gown, grabs his clothes and heads down the stairs to the guest bathroom to shower, which saves him time waiting for Cynthia to finish. He then moves quickly to the kitchen and puts the percolator on. When Cynthia finishes showering and joins Sebastian in the kitchen, she finds a perfect coffee and fruit toast waiting for her.

"Well thank you, darling. What a pleasant surprise!"

Sebastian, still at the toaster awaiting his fill, faces her and sardonically remarks, "What took you so long? A minute later and someone like Paul might have been sitting in your spot enjoying your lovely breakfast." Sebastian chuckles at his own wit and turns back as his breakfast pops up from the toaster.

Even though Cynthia generally has an unfailing ability to deal with Sebastian's idiosyncrasies, her mood suddenly changes. "Let it go, Sebastian! You're a big boy now. Get over it!"

He finishes buttering his toast and parks himself at the table, takes a sip of his coffee and innocently smiles at her. She frowns back at him and he eventually breaks the silence.

"Oh, come on, Cynthia! It was a joke and it was focused on how silly I acted more so than aimed at you," he protests rather weakly.

Cynthia, quite aware of which way his sarcasm was directed, takes advantage of the situation and runs with it. "You're right, Seb. I'm a bit touchy this morning. I should have known that after making this lovely breakfast you wouldn't ruin it with a sarcastic comment towards me."

He looks up from cutting his toast and replies, "Exactly. Just a bit of a joke, that's all."

Cynthia smiles beatifically while slightly tilting her head to the side. "I'm so glad you are **over** Paul arriving when he did and me giving him your breakfast. Sometimes you're more understanding than I give you credit for.

He withdraws his focus from his plate and smiles up at her, "There is nothing to get over, really," he says with some renewed confidence.

Cynthia stirs her coffee and looks into it as if mesmerised by its ripples. Dreamily she says, "I'm very pleased you feel that way, Seb. I was really concerned that it would put your working relationship in jeopardy."

Sebastian's chin cocks back into his throat. "Not at all. I was never really angry with him. No, there was no real issue; I just found my routine out of order, that's all. I actually like the young man, to be honest."

Cynthia smiles as if she is sincerely relieved about his newfound forgiveness. "That's great, Seb. I rather like him too and I think we should ask Paul and his fiancée over for dinner one night."

Sebastian having taken rather a large bite of his toast gags and spits into his napkin, muttering under his breath. Cynthia, grinning like the Cheshire cat, enquires insincerely, "Are you okay, Seb? It seems like you may have bitten off a little more than you can chew."

Outside, a horn toots.

"Paul's here, my love. I have to go," he says with a pasted smile. He kisses her and heads for the door but just before he gets out of the kitchen she calls out to him, "Sebastian!"

He looks over his shoulder, "We will talk about it over dinner tonight but I really have to go now!" he replies, hoping she will have forgotten by then. She straightens her shoulders and glares at him in the motherly way which brings him to an abrupt halt. "Oh come on, Cynthia! I haven't got time to discuss it now!"He says hastily.

She places her hands on her hips and tilts forward like an aggravated hen. "I'm not about to discuss having dinner with Paul and his fiancée at this very moment, although I do intend to remind you later; I wanted to inform you why I arrived later to breakfast than usual this morning. I decided to go back to our room to see if you had remembered your folder, and of course, you hadn't, so I brought it down with me and put it on the hallstand. All I wanted to say to you was, please make sure you grab it on your way out."

Sebastian closes his eyes, bows his head and grimaces. "Thank you, I do appreciate you doing that for me."

Cynthia walks over to him and kisses him on his lowered forehead, then smiles into his eyes while straightening his tie. "Now go or you'll be late." Sebastian heads for the front door and is about to open it when he hears, "Don't forget the folder!" He glides back to the stand as if on ice, grabs the folder and his cane then hurries out the door and to the waiting navy blue sedan.

Paul's sitting patiently in the humming car when Sebastian opens the rear door, flings his folder and cane onto the seat and then plops himself downin the front passenger seat. "Morning Seb," he says with a welcoming smile.

"Good morning Paul. Why didn't you come in for a coffee?"

Paul waits patiently while Sebastian puts on his seatbelt. "I thought it might be a bad idea after yesterday. I know I mess around a bit at times but I really don't want to overstep my boundaries with you."

If Sebastian wasn't feeling down on himself before, he certainly is now. He's already aware his old world, which remained unchanged for so many years, has converted from being confined to research, lecturing and counselling clients to dealing with another world that exists outside of what seems like his normality, so his immediate reaction is to set things right. "Look, Paul, what happened yesterday is dead and buried but what I'd like to do is ask you and your fiancée over for dinner one night so we can all get to know each other a little better."

Paul, driving towards the gates, turns his head slightly. "Okay, I guess."

Sebastian's lip curls on one side. "Well, is that a yes or a no?"

Paul replies, "Yes, Seb, just let me know when. By the way, how did you know I was engaged?"

Feeling he has a 'one up' on Paul, Sebastian becomes mischievous. "Someone mentioned it to me at the station some time back. Anyway, that's irrelevant. I'll talk to Cynthia and arrange a time and date for dinner." He removes his phone from the inside pocket of his jacket and dials Cynthia and lets her know he's invited Paul. She takes a while to respond as she really didn't expect Sebastian to go along with her suggestion but is overjoyed that he has. Arrangements are made for a month's time and Sebastian decides to find out a little more about Paul's fiancée. "Tell me, Paul, where did you and your fiancée meet?"

Paul is still having trouble coming to terms with Sebastian's new found attitude, especially after yesterday's confrontation. He finds the sincerity in Sebastian's voice off-putting and can't help but reply unsurely, "It's a long story, Seb. Why?"

Sebastian, who is always quick to let go of any indiscretions – especially if they are his own – can't understand why Paul seems so apprehensive about answering his question. "Well, I just thought if you and your fiancée are coming over to dinner, I would like to be a little more informed. I'm sure it would enable better communication and make her feel more comfortable."

"Oh, okay. Well, Chelsea is a model and the first time I laid eyes on her was at the airport. She was on a photo shoot for a magazine and I had just finished a tour of Afghanistan. As soon as my plane landed I grabbed my gear and headed straight outside to hail a cab. Once I was outside, the photographer, lighting crew and models were all blocking my path so I told them I needed to get through. The dumbass photographer glared at me and yelled, "IMPOSSIBLE, YOU WILL JUST HAVE TO WAIT!" It had been a long flight and there was a lot of stuff going on in my head, so I brushed past the lighting crew and grabbed him by his shirt and said, "I've seen impossible where I've been and this isn't even close!" I gave him a bit of a shove and kept walking. I was still in my military outfit and Chelsea connected immediately.

Apparently she had lost a cousin after he came back from a long stint in the army in Iraq. I guess he was no longer able to deal with the things he had seen and experienced, so the poor beggar ended it all by jumping off a bridge. At first, I thought Chelsea may have felt sorry for me but the more we saw each other, the more I understood that pity isn't her thing, so I guess in some strange way she felt an affinity with me. Anyway, she grabbed my arm and asked if I would wait for her to finish the shoot, so I did. Later we went for drinks, as she wanted to know what it was like to fight in an unfamiliar place and how that would make her cousin change to the point where he would take his own life. We just seemed to hit it off that day and have been together ever since, although she does spend some long stretches overseas modelling at times."

Sebastian frowns. "I suppose she would. How do you cope with that?"

Paul grins. "Skype, my friend, Skype."

They are only a few blocks from the station now and Sebastian spends the rest of the trip gazing placidly out of the car window, which makes the smooth drive to the office quiet but pleasant.

Outside the station both of them alight simultaneously but just as Paul is about to lock the doors, Sebastian remembers. "**Wait**! I left my folder and cane on the back seat," he bellows and turns back toward the car. Paul crosses his arms, focuses his eyes skyward while moving his head side to side in a disapproving manner. Sebastian snatches his belongings from the rear seat.

Paul is waiting impatiently with pursed lips. "Is there anything else you've left in the car before I lock it?" he snaps cuttingly. Sebastian, still in a positive frame of mind after performing his good deed for the day, thinks that Paul is being courteous. "No but thanks for asking," he replies respectfully, which aggravates Paul even further but he betrays nothing of his true feelings, unsure whether Sebastian is deliberately baiting him.

Sebastian strolls past Paul in a nonchalant manner, then stops and looks back over his shoulder "Are you coming, Paul? Why is it you always seem to be lagging behind?"

Paul sucks in a deep breath, looks skyward again, and then plummets his dead eyes until they focus directly into Sebastian's. "I am so sorry, Seb. I have a bad habit of being ignorant and tardy. I need to work harder on these negative issues. Anyway, you go ahead. I really need to grab myself a coffee as I seem a little distracted this morning and a good espresso may be just the thing I need to pick me up." He retorts sarcastically.

Sebastian, as usual, has his focus on other things and responds, "Good for you, lad. I had a feeling you were having an off day and it takes a real man to admit it." He heads to the station, whistling joyfully. Paul, in turn, fumes off toward the coffee shop at pace.

Sebastian clamps the report between his arm and ribcage, strolls to the reception desk and begins chatting with one of the policemen. Eventually Paul joins him and Sebastian with his cane and folder and Paul sipping his coffee head off to Jim's office. Emily, busily typing away with her earphones on, gets a start when Paul throws a crumpled piece of paper across her desk. "What the

...! Hell, Paul, you scared the living daylights out of me!" she barks, as she pulls her earphones off.

"Sorry Emily. I didn't know what other way to get your attention. Is Jim in?"

Emily, still a little disgruntled, replies disdainfully, "Of course he's in and he wants to see the two of you immediately." She hops out of her chair and announces their arrival.

As they enter, Jim ceases pacing and begins fidgeting with items on his desk.

"What's wrong, Jim? You appear to be out of sorts." Sebastian enquires.

The Chief snaps, "I'll be okay if you wrap up this case quick smart!"

Sebastian has a brilliant mind and there are times where he shows signs of eccentricity but it would show exceptionally bad judgement to underestimate the man's ability to perceive what others see as the unperceivable; so his mouth curls at one corner which, in turn, bends his nose in the same direction. "Okay. So what Is It, Jim? Did the victim have connections in high places? Or more likely, I will say this killer has struck before and you have concerns that he or she will strike again."

As always, Jim finds himself surprised at Sebastian's amazing insight. "We've been going through some of the cold cases and found two more murders that match the format of this one. The Commissioner has asked me to keep a cap on this possibly being a serial killer. We have informed the press that we can't give any details of how the victim was murdered until we have received the Coroner's report which we will delay for as long as possible. The moment that there's any hint of there being a serial killer involved, there's bound to be a public outcry, which in turn leads to pressure coming from above."

Sebastian cuts in, "And you're sitting directly below the political draft so as you said, you want this case cleared up fast."

Jim now sits to attention. "Do you have any clues after viewing the crime scene?"

Sebastian slides his folder across the desk and, in turn, Jim takes a folder from his desk drawer and passes it across to Sebastian. "Now here's the file on the two prior murders. The only thing they had in common is they both frequented the same gym and, judging by the jogging suit our latest victim was wearing, it wouldn't surprise me if he had been there as well."

"I've been asked by the commissioner to set up a task force but I know how you like to interview suspects and witnesses before their thoughts and remarks are inadvertently tainted. I've stalled putting it together momentarily but I can't hold off forever, so I need the two of you on to this, pronto."

Sebastian thanks Jim for having faith in him, grabs the file from his desk and both he and Paul head down the corridor to Sebastian's office, The Dust Pit. On arrival, they pull up a seat opposite each other Paul starts making phone calls to sponsors labelled on the dead man's tracksuit, while Sebastian opens the manilla folder Jim has given him and begins perusing the previous victims' files. The first is a salesman named Nathan Spedding, a single man who only lived in town for a few months before his murder. He had been found in the same manner as the dead man they had seen at the park; only Mr Spedding had been left on a railway station platform not far from Truscan Park. The second, Owen Coleman, was propped up under a tree in a nearby schoolyard overlooking its playground.

After making a number of calls, Paul excitedly declares, "I've got him, Seb! The victim was Mike Cohen and he was about to be selected for the national triathlon team." Sebastian, looking through a magnifying glass at photos from the latest crime scene, raises his eyebrows, tilts his head to one side; Paul knows exactly what that look means and stares up at the ceiling while moving his head from side to side. "Yes Seb, You were right as usual. You were also right when you said it may be a serial killer."

Sebastian puts his magnifying glass down and gives Paul his full focus. "I suggest you inform Jim of this so he can send someone around to notify the next of kin."

Paul rises to his feet. "I'll get onto it now Seb, see you shortly."

Not long after he returns to find Sebastian still folded over his magnifying glass scanning the photos of Michael Cohen's body. "All done, Seb, Jim said he will have someone out to their house within the hour." Sebastian glances up, gives a nod and quickly focuses his eyes back on the photos.

Without warning, he raises his head again and says, "Look at this, Paul!" He holds one of the photos up and continues, "There's a small tattoo of what looks like an insect on the right knee. I thought it was a speck of dirt at first but upon closer inspection I could see it actually has legs. Here, use the magnifier. You'll be able to see it better."

Paul looks carefully at the photo. "I could be wrong, Seb, but it looks like a flea."

"No, I don't think you're wrong at all. I'd say that's exactly what it is and if you look carefully, you'll see it's been cut into the skin."

Paul frowns, "So what are you saying, Seb? Do you believe the killer may have put it there?"

Sebastian peers up. "You know me better than that, Paul. I'm not saying anything, I just state the facts. But it is a possibility and if it is, then this little flea may have a large impact on the case. I think we need to pay Mike Cohen's parents a visit. Paul, would you mind ringing them? Although you may have to make the call a bit later on to give them time to take in what has happened to their son and I think it would certainly be better if the call came from officialdom, wouldn't you agree?"

Paul's eyes flitter back and forth in thought. "So when would you like me to arrange the meeting?"

Sebastian, who has returned to examining the photo, creases his forehead as he looks up, "That's a good question, Paul. I'm sure they will still be fairly incoherent due to the trauma of losing their son but if we don't interview them quickly, vital recollections may be lost. Normally when we lose someone we tend to reflect on the good and bad times that we have had with those who have passed. What we actually need to know about, are others that the deceased has connected or associated with. So the quicker, the better; I think tomorrow morning would be an ideal time."

Paul nods in agreement.

Sebastian rings Cynthia and asks if she can check the financial status of the Cohens as Paul looks through the other victims' files. The morning turns into afternoon and Paul gets on the phone to the Cohens and arranges a meeting for the following morning. "All done Seb; we have to be at the Cohens around nine in the morning".

Sebastian looks up from what he is doing. "Good work, Paul! Now I need to stretch my legs and I think a coffee is in order as well. Can I get you one?"

Paul has his head buried in his computer, checking if there is any criminal history regarding the Cohens and without looking up, replies, "That would be great Seb, I could really go for a pick me up."

Sebastian soon returns with two smoking mugs of coffee and places Paul's on the desk next to him.

"Thanks, Seb. It seems like the Cohens are squeaky clean; apart from a couple of speeding fines but that's about it." Just as Sebastian is about to reply his phone rings and Cynthia is on the other end.

"Hi, Seb."

"Hello, my love. What do you have for me?"

"Well, for a start, Steve and Mary Cohen were guarantors for a sports store that Mike owned and it recently went bust, leaving them in a whole lot of financial trouble."

Sebastian pauses and then responds, "Okay. You said for a start... what else have you found out?"

"You are going to love this; Michael's parents also deposited one hundred thousand dollars into his business account, which was withdrawn by Michael the day after the liquidators notified him they were foreclosing. Once it was official and the auditors went in they could see the anomaly, so they began an investigation immediately. This all happened just prior to Michael Cohen's demise."

"Well, that **is** interesting. What would I do without you, my love?"

As soon as he is off the phone to his wife, he notifies Paul of Cynthia's findings and Paul looks at Sebastian curiously. "So what do you make of that, Seb?"

Sebastian breathes deeply. "I'm not quite sure what to make of it, my friend. It may mean a lot of things but what I do know is I will have to choose the right moment to enquire of Mr Cohen's knowledge of the fact."

Paul crosses his arms, eases gently back into his chair and his face fills with thought. "What if he does know, Seb? Is it possible that he killed his own son in that fashion?"

"Anything is possible, Paul, but don't forget we have two other unanswered murders that were executed in an almost identical fashion. Not one of these killings has been released to the press, so unless Michael Cohen's father was involved in the previous two murders or had knowledge of them, then we can rule him out as a suspect. But it will be hard to know until we speak to him tomorrow, what sort of man he is."

Paul looks down at his crossed arms and gently nods. "I see what you're saying, Seb. It's only early in this case and we need to take it as it comes," he paraphrases in an agreeing manner.

Paul decides to setup a pinboard with photos and background information on it, while Sebastian makes notes to give to Jim at the end of the day. He feels it's important to keep him updated in order to ease his mind with the knowledge that he and Paul are making good progress on the case. The afternoon flies by and they decide to call it a day; while Paul gets the car and coffees to have on the way home, Sebastian drops his update into Jim and lets him know they have arranged an interview with Michael Cohen's parents for the following morning. Once Paul has dropped Sebastian off at home, Sebastian spends time in the study telling his wife about the day's events and after dinner and a nightcap he decides to head upstairs to bed for an early night.

Sebastian is up early and finishing the last morsels of his breakfast when he hears the toot of Paul's car. So he hastily grabs his coat and cane and dashes out the front door to greet him, "Good morning my friend, how are you this fine morning?"

Paul's eyebrows lift with curiosity, "Good?"

Sebastian, with a big smile on his face, nestles back after putting on his seat belt, "Well off we go then,"

Paul accelerates up the drive and quickly glances over to Sebastian, "What's perked you up this morning, Seb?"

Without time to blink an eyelid, Sebastian responds "We are about to begin the hunt in earnest my good man and this is when I really feel alive!" It isn't long before Sebastian's mood washes over Paul and the drive toward the Cohens is filled with contagious enthusiasm.

The Cohen's street is lined with neat timber homes, well-trimmed lawns and hedges and although the pavements are empty at this time of day, Sebastian and Paul can sense the sound of mowers and of children joyfully riding their bikes; as they inhale the distinctive smell of the weekend's freshly cut grass.

They pull up in front of the Cohens and make their way up the stained timber steps to the veranda where Paul knocks on the solid oak door. A short, stoic and exceptionally slim gentleman in his mid to late fifties opens the door and scans Sebastian – who stands there in a magnificently tailored Italian suit while leaning on his dragon-handled cane – up and down. "I'm sorry. I think you may have the wrong house and I wish I could help you but this isn't a good time," he says in a very soft voice and proceeds to close the door.

Paul puts his hand on the door to stop it shutting on them and draws his police badge from his jacket with his other hand. "No, Sir. We have the correct address. I'm Officer Paul Lyon and this is my associate, Mister Sebastian Cork and we have been sent here regarding your son's death. Is there any chance we can come in?"

Cohen sighs deeply. "Of course, you rang yesterday. What was I thinking? I guess I wasn't expecting... oh, never mind. Come in!" He escorts them into a living room where Mrs Cohen sits feebly in an oversized floral armchair. Still clad in a pink velour dressing gown with matching slippers. She has a drawn face and wavy, shoulder-length greying hair, that has yet to be brushed. "Please take a seat on the sofa," Mr Cohen instructs.

Paul knows better than to begin the questioning and leaves it up to his mentor to lead the way. Sebastian believes a mother knows her son better than anyone and, although he can see she is trying to fight off her despair, he focuses his questioning on her. "I'm sorry for your loss, Mrs Cohen, and as much as I hate to ask personal questions regarding your son, the information you provide may help us find his killer."

At first she sits, staring absently, but then her hands tremble and tears flow down her face in torrents. "Why? Why would anybody want to hurt Mike? He was all we had, why would they do this?" she says in a choking voice.

Sebastian loses his professional face and it shades with empathy, "Once we have found the person who did this intolerable act, we will also do our best to find the answers you are seeking."

Her husband sits in silent solace, his eyes moist as he works hard to fight back the tears. Sebastian can see his sufferance but knows he has to continue as time is of the essence. If pressure is put on Jim to hurry along with the task force, Sebastian believes statements from those who knew the victim may be inadvertently suppressed when officers begin to ask questions in the regimented way they are taught to take statements. "Tell me, Mrs Cohen, how did Mike get along with others?"

Mrs Cohen wipes the tears with a handkerchief and rubs her index finger up and down the side of her nose as she answers, "Mike didn't have a lot of friends but those that knew him loved him. Just ask Gail; she will tell you."

Paul chips in "Gail?"

Mrs Cohen sniffles. "Yes. Gail Hartford is Mike's fiancée... or should I say was." Her voice quavers and breaks down again.

Mike's father, quickly moves to his wife's chair, braces his arm around her and looks sullenly at Sebastian. "Gail will be here shortly and I don't think my wife can handle much more today. Would you mind if I take her upstairs so she can have a lie-down? I'll be right back."

Sebastian holds up the palms of both hands. "We fully understand. I wish this questioning weren't necessary. If you wouldn't mind giving us a few minutes of your time once you have taken your wife to her room? I'd like to clear up some issues regarding Mike's financial status." Mrs Cohen begins sobbing inconsolably and her husband's brows meet with torment. "Of course but I really must get my wife upstairs and to bed," he replies tersely. Mr Cohen hunches and half carries his wife up the stairs, as her legs are shaking so badly that she can barely stand.

Paul turns to Sebastian. "Poor beggars; I can't imagine what they're going through. Certainly didn't get much out of that chat."

Sebastian returns his look in a way that acknowledges Paul's empathy. "Not all's lost, Paul. We now know Mike wasn't popular and that tells me he must have created enemies with his negative demeanour and perhaps with his business issues as well."

Paul rotates his head quickly. "Apart from his business problems, how could you possibly know that?"

Sebastian turns up a grin. "She was telling the truth about Mike not having a lot of friends but when she began rubbing her finger up and down her nose, it told me she was either exaggerating or lying when she said those that knew Mike loved him."

As Sebastian finishes explaining, Mr Cohen works his way back into the room. He stares directly into Sebastian's eyes as he reverses into his armchair and responds to Sebastian's earlier statement. "I presume you know about my son's bankruptcy and the financial burden we have now incurred. I'm more than prepared to discuss these issues with you, given the circumstances, but if you accuse me of murdering my own son, you will be asked to leave immediately. Now, what would you like to know?"

Sebastian leans forward, resting his hands on the top of his cane which was resting dormant between his legs and the shroud of empathy has now been removed from his face. "First of all, Mr Cohen, I would like to thank you for being so candid when it comes to discussing your private affairs. Now, down to the job at hand: what did you feel when your son told you he was in financial hot water?"

Steve Cohen blinks, swallows and then allows his sad eyes to meet Sebastian's. "We knew he was having financial difficulties; we just didn't know the extent of it. It came as an absolute shock to find out he declared himself bankrupt a week before his death. I still haven't told Mary, she's way too fragile at the moment and any more bad news could tip her over the edge."

Sebastian slumps back into the seat. "Surely you must have seen it coming? After all, the writing was well and truly on the wall."

Mr Cohen's bottom lip begins to quiver. "No, no definitely not! The writing wasn't there for us! Yes he spoke to me about finances and that he needed a loan to get things back on track, so I lent him one hundred thousand dollars so he could buy stock and trade himself out of debt but when I received a phone call on Monday last week saying that my son had declared himself bankrupt and as guarantors his mother and I were now liable for his debt, I felt numb! I not only lost the nest egg we were saving for our retirement but I also knew we would have to take out an additional loan on our family home."

Sebastian interjects, "That must have also made you angry." He says with sharp eyes.

"Yes, I was angry but who wouldn't be? But he was my son and if only I could do it again, I would. The one thing you must understand Mr Cork, is my son had some very major sponsorships and I knew he would come good on things sooner or later. I tried to ring and talk to him about the issues he was having but he didn't return my calls, so I thought I would leave him alone to give him time to get his head together. Maybe if I'd kept trying, he'd still be alive." He drops his head into his hands and begins to sob.

Sebastian is quick to lean forward again, "Is there anything I can get you?"

Mr Cohen rubs his eyes with the bottom of his hands and slumps back into his chair. "No. I'm fine. I guess I have spent so much of my time being strong for Mary that it finally caught up with me. I'm okay now. Go ahead."

Sebastian looks at him through concerned eyes and gently smiles. "This will be my last question, Mr Cohen, and it may be a difficult one given the circumstances. Did you have any idea your son withdrew one hundred thousand dollars out of the business just prior its liquidation and that he was being investigated for its whereabouts just before his murder?"

Mr Cohen raises his head, he squints inquisitively and the sadness in his eyes turns tense. "What are you talking about? I gave him that money to help get everything back on track! He was going to use it to buy new stock to help him trade out. What the hell is going on? I always thought I knew my son; it seems I never knew him at all. He may not have been perfect but I was always able to trust him. Now I don't know what to think."

Sebastian is quick to reconcile him. "Please, don't jump to conclusions. There could be a number of reasons for the discrepancy and I will let you know when I have investigated the matter further."

Just then the doorbell chimes.

Mike's father leads in a solidly built brunette and introduces her. "This is Gail, Mike's fiancée. Now, if you have no other questions for me, I'd like to go upstairs and be with my wife. Gail, would you mind showing these gentlemen where the tea and coffee is. They may feel like a hot brew."

Sebastian's quick to respond, "No, no we're fine thanks. But I would like to ask some questions, if that's okay with you, Gail."

Gail looks ragged with her red-rimmed eyes and pale complexion. "Yes, of course. I will help in any way I can to make this bastard answerable for the misery he's caused." She takes a seat opposite them and Sebastian opens the questioning.

"First of all Gail, I'm so sorry for your loss. Let us know if you need to stop during the interview."

Gail now seems steady and alert. "I've done my crying and now it's time to do what I need to do to get on top of things. As you can see, Mike's parents aren't handling this too well at all and they need me to be strong for them. They're all I've got now and I'm all they have."

Sebastian pauses briefly, "When you say they're all you've got...?"

"My mother's first husband was infertile and they ended up separating. Then she met my father when she was forty-three and he was fifty-eight. The doctors told my mother that it was a risk having a child at her age but I guess some people have an overriding need; she died giving birth to me. So I never really knew her. Dad, on the other hand, was the greatest parent a child could ever have and he passed last year at the age of eighty-three. I'm so grateful that both Mike and his parents had the opportunity to meet him a year before he died. As for Mike and I, we met two years ago at a party after a triathlon we competed in. Both of us are socially inept and I guess that's why we hit it off."

Sebastian leans back and interlocks his fingers on his belly. "Tell me, Gail, did Mike have many enemies? It seems from what you're saying that he had trouble socially; do you feel this could have led in any way to his demise."

"I guess anything is possible. People didn't see Mike the way I did. Yes, he could be blunt and outspoken. He could also be obnoxious when he was bragging about being better than everyone else. That's why people avoided him. But I saw a different side of him. He was hard on the outside and a kitten on the inside. He worked his heart out to become the best at what he did and never once asked for help. He was generous to a flaw but when it came to competition he was in it to win it. I don't know about enemies but he certainly didn't have a lot of friends."

Sebastian leans forward and stares her in the eyes. "Can you think of anyone who he recently argued with?"

Gail shrugs her shoulders and turns the corner of her mouth up. "There was always something. I mean, he said about some guy down at the gym asking him about his training routine and Mike told him where to get off and there was also a woman down there selling sports drinks; apparently she was keen on him before we became an item but he always said there was nothing between them. I think her name's Kate. I told Mike he needed to tell her that he had a fiancée now but when he did, she started ranting and raving. He was dumbfounded by her reaction as he just saw them as friends and had never seen that side of her. It couldn't have been anything though."

Sebastian, curious, asks, "Why so?"

"Because she apologised the following morning saying she had had an off day. Mike said everything had been fine since that blow-up."

"Just two more questions and we'll wrap it up. Did your fiancée mention anything she'd said during her rant?"

"Only one, and the only reason I remember was he found it amusing when she called him Mister High and Mighty and said he needed cutting down to size. As I said, though, she apologised to him and said she was over it. Mike said there were no hard or uncomfortable feelings between them again."

Sebastian gives her a gentle grin. "Last question... I can see you're an athlete yourself; why didn't you attend the same gym as your fiancée?"

Gail scratches the side of her face and tightens her lips. "We used to but we come to an agreement some time back that we needed to grow as individuals and pursue our own goals. I was a fairly average at triathlons and decided to get into bodybuilding and have done very well for myself since swapping. Mike never cared too much for women with muscles but adjusted once I moved to another gym."

"Okay, that's us for now."

Sebastian and Paul rise off the sofa and Gail rises with them. "Please, let me know if you find out something, won't you?"

Sebastian nods and smiles. "You'll be one of the first to know. Say goodbye to Mike's parents for us."

Back in the car, on their way to the station, Sebastian, who has been staring out of the window in what seems like an hypnotic trance, suddenly swings his head around. "Tell me, Paul, did you notice anything out of the ordinary during our conversation with Gail?"

Paul quickly glances sideways to Sebastian and then back to the traffic ahead. "Like what?"

Sebastian sighs deeply, "If I gave you the answer, there would be no point to my question, now, would there?"

Paul frowns. "Can I be honest with you, Seb?"

"I wouldn't want it any other way. Please go ahead."

Paul tightens his lips. "This is hard, Seb, but I guess it's better to throw all the cards on the table. When I first met you I had no idea of who you really were."

Sebastian looks at him with questioning eyes. "I'm sorry Paul I'm not sure what you mean by who I really was?'

Paul exhales nervously. "Well, I thought you were like one of these profilers or just some sort of basic psychologist, you know, not the real deal; not someone who is internationally noted."

Nothing, from his passenger.

"So, anyway, once I began researching your accomplishments, I started to feel overwhelmed and to say the least, a bit insecure. So I have been trying to hold back when it comes to giving an opinion until I feel I've learnt enough from you to give one that has some substance."

Nothing still. Sebastian crosses his arms, looks to the roof of the car, then brings his eyes back down and simultaneously closes them as he sighs deeply. A few uncomfortable moments pass before he finally opens his eyes and breaks the silence:

"My **goodness,** man! I thought you would be the **last** person in this world who would say something like **that** to me!"

Paul is jolted out of his self-absorption. "Wha- what do you mean?"

Sebastian peers at him through narrowed eyes. "What do I **mean**? I will tell you what I **mean**! Every Tom, Dick and Harry who ever met me or heard of me thought I was some sort of super-genius; do you **know** the pressure that brings on someone to constantly perform at a certain level or even do better? It was a constant bloody **nightmare**, that's what it was!"

"And just when I think I have found my escape from it all, working with someone I admire for their courage overseas in a horrible war and their down to earth characteristics, they turn around and tell me they're overwhelmed by who I am! Now stop the bloody nonsense, make me feel human again and tell me what you bloody well observed!

Paul's brow folds and he remains silent.

"Tell me **something**, Paul, before I make a fool of myself by assuming you have suddenly been struck dumb or perhaps you are bloody well deaf?"

Paul turns with a glazed over stare. "**No**, Seb, I haven't been struck dumb and I haven't lost my hearing either. As for your question, **here** is my answer: Gail seemed unsure about Kate's name as if they'd never met and yet she went to the same gym as Michael and left when they apparently come to an agreement. I'm still not sure that an agreement was reached because she nervously scratched her face when she made that statement, therefore I would imagine they argued over her leaving the gym to pursue her own interests and that she is more familiar with Kate than she is making out."

Sebastian looks out the side window at the scenery. Paul glances over at him at intermittent intervals and eventually exclaims, "Well?"

"Well what?"

Paul rolls his eyes. "Well, how did I do?"

Sebastian, waggling his head from side to side in an exaggerated motion, turns back to watching out the window.

Paul's eyes flash with anger. He swings the car to the curb and brings it to a screeching halt. Sebastian and Paul are jolted forward and only the tension of their seatbelts prevents a couple of very sore heads; then they are flung hard back into their seats. Paul grips the wheel with both white-knuckled hands and Sebastian glares mindfully out the window, still and quiet for what seems like an eternity.

First to break the silence, Paul flicks a venomous stare in Sebastian's direction and hisses "Now you can either answer me or get the hell out of the car and walk the rest of the way!"

Sebastian calmly turns and smiles pleasantly. "Good! Now we are back to some sort of normality... but a little melodramatic, don't you think?"

"What?"

Sebastian strokes the dash while pushing his chin forward. "Melodramatic, you know; over the top?"

Paul's brow wrinkles and he frustratingly splutters, "I know what melodramatic means; that's not what I was asking you about! What did you mean by being back to some sort of normality?"

Sebastian arrogantly grins as he explains. "Well, for a start, who would talk to a world-renowned psychologist in such a manner? Good for you! And secondly, I couldn't have made that deduction any better myself, right down to her body movement indicators."

Paul humbles and looks at Sebastian through admiring eyes. "Seriously, do you think so?"

"No, but it was exceptionally accurate. Now, if you wouldn't mind." He turns his head forward and juts his chin.

Paul indicates, pulls back out into traffic and glances back over at Sebastian. "You really know how to piss people off when you want, don't you?"

Sebastian barely moves a muscle and just the corner of his lip curls as he replies, "Yes."

Paul shakes his head and smiles.

On their return to the Dust Pit, Sebastian remains standing. "If you don't mind, Paul, I will head over to Jim's office and inform him of the details of the interview with the Cohens. Tell me something before I go. When you were in the Special Services, what were your duties?"

Sebastian is in the doorway so Paul swivels to face him. "I had a lot of duties, Seb. Armed and unarmed combat, surveillance..."

"Yes, surveillance, so you used maps and the like?"

"All the time; we needed to know how to locate the enemy or find our way back if we were ever separated from the platoon. Why?"

Sebastian rubs his chin. "Well, I was hoping that tomorrow we might try and find where these murders took place."

Paul places his hands behind his head and pushes back into his chair confidently. "So you want me to scan over some maps in order to find a possible location?"

"Yes, would you mind?"

"No, not at all. But I won't be able to get much done until tonight. I still have a bit to finish here before we leave, so I better get onto it."He drops his arms and swivels around to the desk.

Sebastian acknowledges Paul's needs and begins his walk up to Jim's office where Emily announces him.

"I read yesterday's report, Seb, and I have to say great job to the pair of you in finding out who the victim was so quickly. I rang the Commissioner and explained that you were on the case and the progress you had already made. I also explained that if we form a task force right now it may hinder your progress, so he has decided to hold off for now. But he said if I didn't keep him updated or provide proof that the case was achieving substantial inroads, he would have to insist the task force be put in place. So I hope you see this more as a positive result than a negative one."

Sebastian nods agreeably. "Definitely Jim; it's nice to know we have that kind of support." He hands the Captain his report. "The other thing is, Paul and I were hoping to take tomorrow to see if we can locate where the murders were committed."

Jim nods with his chin out. "Great idea, Seb, but please be very careful. If you see anything vaguely suspicious, get Paul to call it in and wait for back up. I mean it, Seb! I don't want any heroics from either of you!"

Sebastian grins. "Trust me, Jim, I am no hero and have no intentions of putting myself in any peril whatsoever."

When Sebastian arrives back at the Dust Pit, he brings Paul up to date on his meeting with Jim. Then Paul waits patiently until Sebastian has packed his papers and collected his cane so they can head down to the car together. Paul turns the motor over but before he drives off he looks at Sebastian with a smile. "I've been thinking about our conversation earlier today and I appreciate what you said about how people saw you differently and how hard it was to live up to others expectations. It definitely made me think about how I should approach you in the future."

Sebastian exhales deeply with annoyance. "Seriously, Paul, I feel like you have totally missed the point I was making!" If you have to consider how you will approach me in the future, rather than be yourself, then I have failed miserably in what I have attempted to communicate to you. Oh, by the way... I never quit what I was doing because of the pressure. I quit because I achieved all I could and became bored. So it was more about the adrenaline rush than the pressure I was under. Everything else I said was true, but I will often alter perspectives to make a point."

Paul's eyes bounce around like a pinball. "Well I certainly understand your point now but how do I know you aren't altering the perspective of this conversation to make another point?"

"You don't. Can we go now?" He says as he turns his head to the side window.

The engine throbs a minute longer.

"No! We can't! You want me to be myself, so that's what I'm going to do, but in return I want something from you"

Sebastian impatiently turns to face Paul "And what would that be, my friend?" he conveys sarcastically.

Paul looks him in the eyes with purpose. "I want you to try and remember that you haven't always possessed the perfect gift you have now; it took years to hone it."

Paul sits staring at Sebastian for an uncomfortable moment, thenengages the motor and begins the drive home. Sebastian remains solemn and silent along the way. On reaching his house he collects his belongings from the back of the car and peers over at Paul. "I'll see you in the morning. Oh, by the way... point taken and condition accepted!" The rear door closes.

Sebastian makes his way halfway up the path to where Cynthia awaits him, "You really should ask Paul in for a coffee now and then, Seb."

Sebastian greets his wife with a smile. "Yes, I think you are quite right and do you know something else, my love?" he bows his head and kisses her on the forehead, gazes straight into her eyes. "I think he is a fine young man with a lot of potential."

Cynthia grins lovingly. "I knew you would come around sooner or later."

He looks curiously at her. "What do you mean?"

She smiles warmly into his eyes, "Men don't always see what women do, you know? That young man looks up to you as a father figure."

Sebastian's head tilts to one side. "Do you really think so?"

Cynthia gently shakes her head. "No, Seb. I know so. Now, come on, there's a drink waiting in the study." She tows him down the hallway and then leaves him, to check on dinner. The fire in the study is comforting and burns with a mild incandescence and on her return she finds Sebastian sitting drowsily in his leather chair neither awake nor asleep. "Come on, old man. Dinner is served" He looks up at her with an intoxicated smile and rises to his feet. After dinner Sebastian catches an early night.

The following morning brings a contradictive day with the sun seemingly warmer than normal until the breeze whips up a crisp and arctic chill. Sebastian is feasting on a hearty breakfast that Cynthia has just dished up for him when Paul arrives earlier than expected and gives a sharp toot of the horn.

"You told me last night I should ask him in for coffee, so that is exactly what I will do; after all, I certainly won't let this delicious French toast go to waste," Sebastian says determinedly while rising from the table.

Cynthia smiles as he lumbers out the front and retrieves his partner from the awaiting vehicle. By the time they get back into the kitchen she has already poured an extra coffee and begun frying bread in the pan. "Good morning, Paul. Breakfast won't be long," she says looking over her shoulder from the stove.

Paul holds both his palms outward, "It's okay Mrs Cork, I have already had my breakfast and I'm sure Seb could go another round."

"Nonsense, Paul, it's only French toast. And I told you before not to call me Mrs Cork; my name is Cynthia!"

Paul looks to Sebastian for support.

"Well, don't look at me, Paul; I'm not going to argue in your defence. If you know what is good for you, you'll take a seat and enjoy whatever Cynthia dishes up."

Cynthia's eyes abruptly divert from Paul to Sebastian, "What's that supposed to mean Seb?"

Nothing at all my love, I am just trying to encourage the young man to eat, that's all."

Sebastian moves his plate one chair down. "There you go, my good man. Sit here!"

Paul looks at him uncertainly. "But that's your seat, Seb."

With Cynthia focusing on her cooking, Sebastian motions with his hands impatiently for Paul to sit down. It's not long before she joins them at the table. "Tell me something, Paul. How are you coping with my husband's antics?"

Sebastian, who is about to take a gulp of coffee, places his mug back down and frowns at her with squinting eyes. "What do you mean by my 'antics'?"

Cynthia takes a bite of her breakfast and takes her time to respond. "Perhaps the word I should have used is 'idiosyncrasies'."

Sebastian picks up his mug, only, this time, he partakes in the aromatic brew, then places it down to continue a conversation probably better left alone. "I love that word, 'idiosyncrasies', but I'm not quite certain of its definition. Tell me, Cynthia, does that mean 'personal peculiarities'? You know, like brushing one's hair exactly ten times on each side, or stirring one's coffee three times one way and four the other? Oh yes, then there's the toilet paper…"

"Sebastian, that's enough!" Cynthia snaps with her eyebrows clenched.

Paul is quick to intervene, "Ah, to answer your question, Cynthia, I haven't been coping quite that well and I noticed my idiosyncrasies are causing Sebastian some problems as well but when you are partnering someone you both have to work hard to understand the other's traits."

Sebastian and Cynthia look like pupils who have just been caught flicking paper at each other and go about the rest of the meal in a more respectful manner. Once breakfast is out the way, Cynthia sees them both to the front door. "Here's your cane, Seb. I want you to be careful today, do you hear me?"

Sebastian kisses her on the forehead. "Loud and clear my love; loud and clear!"

Then she turns her attention to Paul. "Make sure you bring him back in one piece, won't you? And take care of yourself too."

He smiles respectfully at her. "You know I will, Cynthia."

She smiles back, "Yes I believe you will."

As they travel through the city they are dwarfed by the massive buildings looming on both sides of them. The haze and smell of fuel predominates but to their surprise the traffic remains unusually steady. Paul, quite proud of himself, explains how diligently he worked the previous evening, mapping out areas that should coincide with the distance travelled by the killer to Truscan Park.

The first half of their day is spent investigating sites in and around the suburbs. They search in and out of abandoned warehouses on the docks for any sign of recent use but all they come across is musky, dank ruins, where whispering winds creep in intermittent puffs through shattered windows in the lofts. Glowing particles of dust dance erratically in the concentrated beams of light, gently but persistently forcing their way deeper into the depths of the murky shadows below. In all the corrugated towering buildings they search the only inhabitants, congregated in the soiled debris that has accumulated over years of neglect are rats, pigeons, spiders and the odd feral cat. Sebastian and Paul use the early afternoon to move from the docks to the outer suburbs' industrial areas but eventually reach the conclusion that none of these are plausible murder sites due to their proximity to other buildings and amount of pedestrian and vehicle traffic. There's no doubt in their minds just how difficult it would be to move a body in or out of these congested roads and pavements without someone noticing or questioning the culprit's motives.

The long morning has turned into late afternoon and as the sun wearies; their search takes them outside the city limits where the bushland is dense. During their tedious journey they catch sight of the odd farm through the breaks in the trees, scattered here and there, far and few between. Many of the paths they drive down become inaccessible or serve up no evidence of suspicious activities. They motor down an unpaved road and the blend of dust and pine works its way through the vents, leaving them with an ashen taste in their mouths and throats. Worse, like all the others, it seems to be taking them nowhere. Sebastian becomes frustrated and weary, "There's no sign of what we are seeking here, so can we search for somewhere to turn around and begin our journey home?"

A look of disappointment falls over Paul's face. "I just don't get it! I went over and over a map of all the areas last night and this was the most promising of them all!"

Sebastian lifts his chin and stares fixedly at the road ahead. "Just a moment Paul. Is that a driveway to the right up there?"

The possibility of vindication within his grasp, Paul ascends the winding, private road bounded either side by dense bush. They come into sight of the remnants of an old homestead burnt to the ground. There's no sign of blackening to the surrounding shrub, so it seems the fire was isolated to the building alone and any other materials, apart from rusting metal that had escaped the intense heat of the fire, have been expunged forever by the elements. A distance from the burnt out remains stands an old red barn made of timber which was most likely collected from the surrounding forest. As they alight from the car Sebastian points with his walking stick. "It may be worth taking a look in there but be careful."

Paul nods and then responds by drawing his gun from its holster and moving with stealth towards the building. Dusk is closing fast and the dappled sunlight filters through the trees in a way that makes Sebastian flinch with a sense of insecurity. A floating cobweb brushes his face, sending a tingle down his spine. He convulses with a shiver and feels a pounding pressure in his ears as his instinctive fear is now overwhelming. He stands and listens to the eerie rustling as the wind flutters the leaves on the bushes around him and he casts an anxious glance towards them. Sebastian decides it may be safer if he walks away from the barn toward open ground; if anything or anybody is to come out of the shrub toward him, he feels he will have clear sight of them and time to ready himself for battle.

Even though his family were farmers Sebastian lost his affinity to the land when he was eight years old. His parents had emigrated from England the previous year and like any boy of his age, he loved to explore but this time he wandered too far. The thoughts of being lost in the forest for two nights are back, vivid and overwhelming. Suddenly he senses that something is lurking behind him. His eyes grow in terror and his expression tightens as he freezes rigid, chills running down his spine like ice water. Then, when a twig snaps his reflexes are sharp and he whirls his body around, his cane held high in readiness to bring it hurtling down on whomever or whatever has snuck up behind him.

Just as he's about to release all the force that flows through his body like electricity, a large figure throws his palms outward in an effort to deflect the blow that would surely crush his skull. "Whoa, Seb! It's me, it's me!"

Sebastian, hyperventilating, his eyes fixed and bulging with frenzied fear, is momentarily numbed by Paul's words.

Paul has seen this response before from soldiers who had witnessed more than their minds could handle. "It's okay, Seb, it's me. I'm sorry. I didn't mean to startle you." Sebastian closes his eyes and inhales some very deep breaths. Still muted with fright, he opens them again and stares fixedly at Paul. "I'm really sorry, Seb. I thought you heard me coming. Are you okay?" Paul slowly lowers his hands.

Sebastian, visibly shaken and with trembling hands, collects himself when he sees Paul is genuinely worried about him. "It's okay, Paul. You just gave me a bit of a start, that's all. I should have been more focused but my mind was somewhere else. Thanks for your concern."

Paul sees Sebastian is embarrassed by his own reactions and rapidly changes the subject. "Anyway, Seb, I searched the entirety of the barn including the loft and found nothing of interest. Do you want to come and have a quick look before it gets dark? He licks his dry lips nods and then hesitantly follows Paul in.

The barn smells damp and musty. A moulding mass of hay lays heavy in the corner of the otherwise vast deserted interior. The last rays of the sun, beam through the loft window illuminating small particles of dust that drift in the stale air. Sebastian moves directly to the middle of the barn and slowly turns clockwise, pausing intermittently. His eyes move up and down and side to side as he scans every square inch of his surrounds. Paul squints at him curiously. "What are you looking for, Seb?"

Sebastian, emotionally inert and still scanning, replies, "You would do better to ask me what I'm not looking for."

Paul shakes his head from side to side rapidly and one side of his mouth turns as if he's making an effort to sustain a wink. "Okay, I'll run with that. What are you not looking for?"he sarcastically replies.

Sebastian points to one corner of the barn at the rear, then over to the other. "That and that," he says and then continues, "I'm not looking for old building materials; I would rather find something new. See those steel girders over there?"

Paul's eyes follow in that direction.

"They're not old at all. Therefore someone has renovated this barn not so long ago. Now why would you do that? If you were going to spend money on this property, wouldn't it be on the house? It's not as though they have any livestock or are using it to dwell in. There are no bedding or kitchen utensils."

Paul can see that Sebastian has hit upon a very good point and replies, "Although, there are some old bicycle tracks over here."

Sebastian remains tight-lipped but walks forward, gently pushing small remnants of hay to one side with his cane. "Oh yes, there. I can see them. You're quite right, Paul, that is interesting."He cuffs both hands over the top of his cane and squats down for a closer look, almost losing his balance in the process. Sebastian reaches one hand into his jacket pocket, draws out a small knife and without opening the blade, places the handle across the tyre track.

Paul squats down also. "So, what do you make of them, Seb?"

Although Paul speaks directly to him, Sebastian's thoughts are far away; he continues staring at the centre of the knife while moving his head to the left and beyond it, then slowly back and to the right and beyond it. "Ah ha!" he declares and quickly places the knife back in his pocket and nonchalantly glances over at Paul. "Like you said, they're tyre tracks but it's way too soon to know if they have anything to do with these murders. I think I am going to have to make another journey up here at some point."

Without seeing any reason to linger or utter another word, Sebastian pushes down hard on the top of his cane to bring himself to his feet, makes a 'Mmm' sound, brings his cane up to rest on his shoulder and starts heading out of the barn. It is only at the entrance it occurs to him that he has forgotten something or someone. While still squatting like a chicken about to lay an egg, Paul remains stationary; a blank look veils his face as he waits impatiently for what Sebastian has in mind to do next.

"We have seen all we need to see here, my friend, so I suggest we head home. I will ask Cynthia to make some enquiries regarding the ownership of the building and we will see where that leads us. By the way, great job on finding this site, Paul. It may turn out to be vital to the investigation." His words only appease Paul somewhat and Paul's joyless reply reflects his disinterest.

"Thanks, Seb."

Sebastian's shadow precedes him as he leaves the barn. The dull green of the bush has now faded into grey silhouettes. Paul continues past Sebastian to the car as he hesitates for a brief moment to focus through a break in the trees where he can see the sun's last rays igniting the horizon like a forest fire across the valley. Before he gets in the car he takes one last hesitant glance over his shoulder at the surrounds when the woods echo eerily with the hoots of an owl.

He sinks comfortably into his seat as Paul starts up the motor to begin their journey back down the old dirt road and it's only a matter of moments 'til shades of grey turn to black masses, while eerie flashes of shrubs are lit up by the headlights leading the way. This weighs heavily on the lids of Sebastian's tired eyes, while the warmth inside the vehicle appeases his fears and insecurities and he's soon fast asleep.

It seems like only a matter of moments to him when he is abruptly woken by a vice-like grip on his arm. "Only a block to go, Seb. Are you awake?"

Sebastian, slowly and semi-conscious, turns his head. "No, Paul, I always sleep through someone vigorously shaking me and idiotically asking if I'm awake. Of course I'm bloody well awake!" He looks down at his arm, where Paul's rather large hand still clings like a possum to a sapling. Then his fiery eyes shoot up to meet Paul's "Now, if you wouldn't mind unleashing me so I can regain some sort of feeling back into my lower forearm and hand, I would be ever so grateful!"

Paul's hand retracts to the steering wheel from whence it came. His eyes are focused steadfast on the road but he's clearly annoyed. "Well that's a little ungrateful, isn't it?"

Sebastian rolls his eyes and crosses his arms as his chin turns unwillingly toward Paul. "What do you mean?"

Paul remains rigid and focused on his driving. "Well, anyone else would have woken you earlier but being the considerate guy I am, I gave you the opportunity to get some rest before we arrive back at your house." Paul glances sharply over to Sebastian and continues, "After all, who else would put up with that noise while they're driving?"

Sebastian's forehead folds like a well-ploughed field and his eyebrows move to introduce themselves. "I beg your pardon! What noise?"

Paul grins inwardly knowing he has thrown out the bait and the hook are about to be set. "You're kidding me, right? Surely Cynthia must complain about your snoring... or do you sleep in separate rooms? Not that it would make a lot of difference."

Sebastian's eyes open wide and he fixes a venomous gaze as he retorts, "No we do not! Not that it has anything to do with you. And no, she hasn't commented on my snoring... because I don't bloody well snore."

They round the corner and pull into Sebastian's driveway and he's quick to get out. He bends down before closing the door and abruptly says, "I will see you tomorrow Paul!"

Paul flashes a cheeky grin and replies, "I've got something I need to do first thing in the morning, so I won't be able to pick you up, Seb. Sorry about that."

Sebastian just gives off a deep grumble.

Paul feels an urge for some additional sarcasm and finishes off the day with, "Sleep well, my friend... because I'm sure there are a lot of people in your neighbourhood who won't!"

Sebastian slams the door shut and marches briskly up the driveway while Paul drives off with a beaming smile across his face. Cynthia has heard the car pull up and the door slam, so she waits anxiously at the entrance.

"Are you okay?" she enquires with a concerned gaze.

He gives his wife her habitual greeting kiss but the conversation with Paul is still fresh in his mind, so Sebastian continues his march into the house with her trailing behind.

"Stop right there, Sebastian Cork; what the heck is going on?"

He looks around at her as a child would their mother. "Do I snore?"

She looks askance at him. "What?"

"Do I bloody snore?"

Cynthia has drawn a mental blank. She can't work out what snoring has to do with the mood he's come home in and stares at him blankly. Sebastian becomes more and more frustrated. "Well, my goodness! Here stands a woman who has an IQ of one hundred and thirty, who topped her class every year at university and yet is stumped with a simple question. Well, butter my bread on both sides! Will miracles never cease?"

Sebastian begins to realise he has overstepped his boundaries and knows the repercussions that are about to rain down on him can't be good. Cynthia crosses her arms and tightens her lips. "Of course you snore, Sebastian. In fact, do you remember Mrs Chalmers who used to live next door?" she says, every inch the lawyer.

"Yes," he replies meekly.

Her eyes, flash with pure determination, as she makes her point, "Well, why do think she moved out?"

Sebastian's heart sinks. "Was it because of my snoring?"

"**No**! Because she was **eighty-nine** years old and her children put her in a bloody home; what a **stupid** answer from a man that topped all his classes in psychology and has an IQ of one hundred and fifty!"

"The reason I didn't answer your question initially is I was stunned by it. Don't you think that at some stage during our many, many... **many** years of marital bliss, I would have informed you if you were a snorer? Where the heck did you get this ridiculous notion from?"

Sebastian, embarrassed to have been taken in so easily, decides not to disclose any further.

"Oh, um, I don't know. Somebody from the station was talking about it and I guess I began to wonder. As far as being snappy, I sincerely apologise, my love. It's been a big day and I guess I'm a little tired, so I truly am very sorry."

Later that evening after dinner, Sebastian and Cynthia head to the study where they often have a quiet drink and discuss the day's events. "You were unusually quiet at dinner tonight Seb; is there something wrong?"

Sebastian takes a long gulp of Bourbon. "No, all is good my love, just a very tiring day, that's all."

"You still haven't told me if you and Paul located a site where the murders may have taken place."

Sebastian pauses. "We found a place that has some possibilities; it's just outside the city in fairly dense bushland. I was hoping if you had a spare moment tomorrow, you might make some phone calls in the morning to see if you can find out who owns the property."

Cynthia finishes her sherry and rises to her feet. "That won't be a problem. Just leave the details for me and I will follow that up for you. But for now, I'm going to have an early night. Are you coming?"

"I really am indecisive about what I should do; there's an interesting documentary I'd like to see but I also have an early start tomorrow. So perhaps I will just watch some of it and turn in when I tire."

"Well, Seb, you're old enough to know what is required, so I will love you and leave you. Oh, by the way, do you want me to set the alarm?"

"No, no I will do that when I come up. And I will try my hardest not to wake you in the morning."

She rinses her glass and places it back in the cabinet. "Goodnight, my darling," she whispers as she bends forward and gently kisses him on the lips. Sebastian finishes off his drink on his way to the cabinet to pour himself another.

Sebastian becomes enthralled in the program and time escapes him until the show eventually concludes, "Oh my goodness, is it really that late?" he mutters to himself as he turns off the TV and gingerly rises to his feet. He remembers he still has to write down the address of the property and he knows if he doesn't do it now he will most certainly forget in the morning. So Sebastian shuffles his way to his office while rubbing his eyes, he writes it down and works his way back to the kitchen where he leaves it on the bench. Sebastian thinks about a cocoa, but better judgement kicks in and he decides bed is a much better option.

Between silk sheets, he closes his eyes momentarily until the dark memories from childhood spring forward like a clown in a music box. Sebastian stirs restlessly and his uneasiness lingers throughout the night as savage eyes and blood-curdling howls from wild dogs of a childhood past, arise from the pitch black corners of his mind. In the early hours of the morning his eyelids slowly close and his mind finds peace as it eventually shuts down into a deep slumber.

Sebastian feels like he has only just closed his eyes when he's woken by Cynthia who is busily working her way around each of the bedroom windows, hauling on the cords to let the sun's torturous ray's burn into his more than sensitive eyes. His first reaction is to throw both his arms across his face like a vampire exposed. "What the heck are you doing, woman?"he growls indignantly from the lack of sleep and nervous strain.

Cynthia, fully dressed, stands over him with her hands on her hips and a straight face. "What do you mean, what am I doing? Wasn't it **you** who said you needed to be downtown early? Wasn't it **you** who said you'd try not to wake me when you leave? And wasn't it **you** who was going to set the alarm? Well, guess what? **You** didn't! And now you need to get a move on if you still want to be in early. So what I suggest is you shift your grumpy bum out of bed and get a hustle on!"

Sebastian throws the sheets off and catapults himself towards the shower. "How late am I?" he says, tripping and stumbling while he tries to remove his pyjama pants.

Cynthia follows close behind picking up his discarded night clothes. "It's alright, Seb. I'm sure you will make it in time. There's a piece of toast waiting in the warmer for you and I'll have a coffee ready to go. Calm down or you will only get in your own way."

When Sebastian has finished showering, he finds all his clothes for the day laid out on the bed so he quickly dresses, heads down the stairs and finds Cynthia waiting with his toast and coffee at the bottom.

"I know I am a complete pain in the 'proverbial' sometimes but don't ever get the notion that I don't appreciate everything you do for me," he kisses her lovingly on the forehead.

Cynthia gives him a beguiling smile as her eyes become deeply entrenched in his and she finds herself going weak at the knees. But she is soon brought back to reality when Sebastian destroys the moment by snatching the goodies out of her hands – 'no time for idle chit-chat, have to rush, love you!' – and racing out the door.

Cynthia strolls into the kitchen for a relaxing coffee. She takes a deep breath and murmurs, "Oh, thank goodness for time alone!" Then the front door opens again and a deep voice reverberates down the hall. "In case you didn't notice, if you look on the kitchen bench, I have left an address and I am hoping you can find out who owns that site; bye!" The door slams shut once more.

The drive to the station is rapid and on arrival Sebastian scurries up the concrete steps, still drinking his morning coffee from a cardboard cup that Cynthia keeps in the kitchen for such occasions. Although he has got off to a slow start, he has beaten the odds by reaching the station early and hopes to get some phone calls out of the way before working through many of the other things he has planned. After wishing the policeman on reception a good morning, he walks at a quick pace toward Jim's office.

"Good morning, Emily, I'm just letting you know I'm here. Have you seen Paul?"he enquires politely.

Emily raises her eyes abruptly from her computer. "No he hasn't checked in yet but Cameron asked if you would drop down and see him."

Sebastian's plans for the morning haven't allowed for this type of distraction and he drops both his head and his lip, knowing whenever the Coroner wants to see you; he more than likely has some vital information which requires your immediate attention. "Did it sound urgent?"

Emily looks at him with a frown. "What do you think?"

Sebastian tries to make light. "You know, Emily, you should never answer a question with a question!"

Always busy at this time of morning, Emily bites her lip in vexation. "And you should know better than to ask a question that you already have the answer to!"

Sebastian's eyes roll upwards, aware that her statement has cleverly counteracted his, "Very good point Emily, my apologies."

Sebastian makes his way downstairs, past the morgue to Cameron's office and finds him busily working on his notes. "Good morning Cameron, what have you got for me?"

Without lifting his head, Cameron replies, "Won't be a moment, Seb. Grab a seat while I just finish up."

Sebastian grimaces with annoyance; he had assumed Cameron would be ready and waiting for him. A few more minutes pass and Cameron throws his pen on the desk, pushes back in his chair and crosses his arms. "I have something for you, Seb."

Sebastian still annoyed abruptly responds, "Yes, Emily told me as such. What is it?"

Cameron gives him a long cool stare and places his hands either side of his desk as if bracing himself for a collision. He clears his throat, frowns and squints. "Get out of the wrong side of bed, did we?"

Silence.

Cameron leans forward and cups his hands. "Well, hopefully, my news will cheer you up and give you something more to go on with this young man's murder. You were quite right asking me to check for a sedative in the victim's stomach. What I actually found was a substance called Ketamine hydrochloride... also known on the streets as super acid, ket and various other names. Ket is a drug that comes in a white powder form, tablet or liquid and is dropped into unsuspecting victim's drinks at bars."

Sebastian's eyes look fixedly at Cameron. "Are you saying the killer is knocking the victims out with a date drug?"

Cameron tightens his lips. "That's exactly what I'm saying, Seb. Ketamine is a disassociate anaesthetic that impacts on the central nervous system. The effects begin within ten to twenty minutes and rapists like it because it can induce some memory loss. Other symptoms can incorporate slurred speech, breathing problems, dissociation, paranoia and hallucinations. In this instance, I think it was the liquid form of the drug as there were traces of it in a sports energy drink we tested from the contents of his stomach."

There's a prolonged silence as Sebastian gives the matter his earnest consideration.

"Are you still with me Seb?"

"Yes, this is very informative. It tells me the killer, either needed to know or be in close vicinity of the victim in order to give him the drug without creating suspicion and I have a good idea where it may have been given to him without his knowledge."

"From what you are saying, Cameron, the perpetrator would have a very limited timeframe to ensure they were alone with the victim after the drug had been consumed. As you pointed out, ten to twenty minutes would be all the time the killer had to get our victim away from prying eyes and into a vehicle and that's no easy task in itself. Someone walking from a bar with a staggering man may be acceptable but from anywhere else, bystanders would ask questions and that's something the killer would want to avoid at all costs."

Cameron raises his eyebrows. "Aren't you jumping the gun a little, Seb? I mean what makes you think the victim wasn't leaving the bar? After all, I never said there wasn't any alcohol in his system."

Sebastian lounges back confidently, crosses his arms, bites gently on his bottom lip and replies, "Two reasons, my friend; firstly, I have seen enough to convince me this young man was in training at the time of his demise and that he competed at the highest level; from my brief experience as a sports psychologist, I would find it difficult to believe that an athlete of his calibre would frequent a bar while preparing for a major event. Secondly, you said yourself the drug was induced by way of a sports drink; how many bars do you know serve an athlete-grade energy drink?"

Cameron smiles and respectfully answers, "There is no doubt you're going to serve us all well here, Seb. I'm sorry I haven't got more time to talk but I really must get back into it"

Sebastian heads back upstairs and on his way to the Dust Pit he catches a glimpse of Paul weaving in and out of the other detectives' desks.

"Good morning, Seb. Did you sleep well?"

Sebastian's lips curl in an indignant manner, "If that was an attempt at sarcasm and you actually meant 'did I snore?' the answer is no! I didn't!"

Paul waves his head from one side to the other with his eyes half shut. "Come on, Seb! It's a new day and I was actually being sincere. Anyway, I got you this on my way in." Paul hands him a coffee and they both sit down at the desk.

"Well! I must say, Paul, this really is a delightful coffee."

Sebastian relays what the Coroner has concluded about the sedative in the sports drink.

"We really need to pay a visit to Michael's gym and I was thinking that we might get more achieved if you operate undercover and I investigate openly for the Police. Once or twice a week, we can meet up here to discuss our progress. If you're happy with my idea, I will arrange an interview first thing tomorrow with the gym owner and, if I'm convinced he has had nothing to do with the murders, I will request he treat you as he would any other patron. I thought you might pop up the corridor and speak to Jim about our plans." Sebastian suggests.

Paul screws the corner of his mouth up thoughtfully and unwittingly mimics Sebastian by crossing his arms as well. "Sounds like a plan. I'll go and have a word with him now."

When Sebastian turns his phone on he receives a barrage of messages from Cynthia asking him to ring her as soon as possible.

"Hello, my love. I am so sorry I haven't got back to you. I was called into the Coroner's office as soon as I arrived and I turned off my phone and forgot to turn it back on. I am so sorry."

There is complete silence at the other end.

"Hello Cynthia, are you there? Hello Cynthia, are you alright?" He glances down at his phone and can see she hasn't hung up, so he begins to panic.

"Cynthia, are you okay?"

The silence is finally broken with sarcasm. "I'm fine why? Did you worry because I didn't answer?"

Sebastian's eyes narrow as he exhales strongly from his nose and his tone becomes stern, "Thankyou Cynthia, I am really pleased you accepted my apology. Now how can I be of service?"

"It's my turn to apologise Seb. I began to worry when you didn't answer my calls. I even contacted Jim to see if you were there."

"Apology accepted my love and I will try not to be so absent minded in the future. Now what is it that was so urgent?"

Cynthia pauses. "Last night you asked me to find out who owns the property and I know you're going to be surprised when I tell you it was recently purchased by Steve Cohen, Mike Cohen's father."

Sebastian's eyes become sharp, "Surely you're not still playing games with me are you, Cynthia?"

"Not at all, I'm very serious!"

He quietly weighs up this new information. "Well, this is certainly putting the cat among the pigeons. I am going to need some time to consider what strategies to put in place. For a start if he is alerted to the fact that we know about this and that he has had something to do with his son's demise, then he will be more on his guard when answering questions. I think I will do a little more delving before we open Pandora's Box. Thank you for this information, my love; it's given me a lot to think about."

"You're welcome Seb. While I have you I was wondering if you are going to be home late tonight. If you are, I will hold off on dinner."

"No-no, I will be home at the usual time."

"Alright; I will let you go now and I will see you when you get home."

Just as he hangs up, Paul enters enthusiastically. "We've got the go ahead of Jim, Seb! Oh, by the way, Jim asked me to let you know, Cynthia has been trying to call you."

Sebastian explains about his phone being off and Paul intuitively feels there is something more bothering Sebastian.

"What's going on Seb you seem out of sorts; is Cynthia alright?"

Sebastian fills Paul in on the new information he has just received.

"That sounds a bit suspicious don't you think. Perhaps we should return to the Cohen's house and ask some questions."

"Let's not jump to any conclusions Paul. Mike may have been visiting the site when he was murdered and his father may still be oblivious that it possibly occurred on his property. We need to go about the investigation the way we planned. If he has got something to do with his son's murder we need to take him by surprise. The only way to do that is to eliminate other suspects."

More things can be hidden, both consciously and sub-consciously, when someone is confronted with hard facts but if one behaves in a manner that avoids confrontation, then the information becomes overt to the enquirer."

Paul listens intently. "As much as I can grasp the concept of what you're telling me, Seb, it will take some time to put it into practice. I will have to unlearn all the interrogation methods used in the Special Services as well as what I have been taught since joining the force. So you will have to be patient with me."

Sebastian smiles. "Whatever you do, Paul, don't unlearn anything. Everything we are taught in life serves a purpose if used at the appropriate time and put in its proper perspective."

The rest of the day is spent ploughing through files and photos and ringing friends and relatives of the victims.

The drive home is routine apart from a quick call from Cameron who fills him in with a few facts that he had already considered. Sebastian walks through the door and hears a faint voice from down the hallway, "I'm here in the study, Seb." So he hangs his coat, places his walking stick in the hallstand and makes his way to where his wife awaits him.

Cynthia is sipping on a sherry while luxuriously relaxed across the chair. She has one leg dangling over the cushioned arm and the other framed upward, supporting her book. They give each other the customary welcoming kiss. "Dinner is on the table. I will be out as soon as I finish the last few lines."

He stands there with an amused smile, pleased to see her so relaxed. It takes him back to their days at university when she would sit under a tree reading and he would secretly admire her from a distance. "If it's okay with you, I might have bourbon and relax before dinner, my love." She glances up and gives him a beguiling smile and then buries her thoughts back into her book.

It's a cool night so Sebastian moves quietly to the fireplace, turns up the heat and then fixes himself a drink. It's not long before the bourbon and the warmth of the room sees him fast asleep in his more than comfortable chair.

It's pitch black in the bedroom when the alarm sounds at five the following morning and, in slapping it – hard –Sebastian knocks the clock clean off his bedside table. His drowsy awareness is now bright and alert, as he flings himself onto the shag pile carpet and searches on hands and knees for the clock's red flashing figures. "Ah, there you are, you slippery little devil!" he extends his arm under the bed but his efforts are to no avail. The clock has somehow twisted its cord around the leg of the bed and Cynthia is awoken from a deep sleep by the constant buzzing, which is penetrating her every nerve cell.

"Sebastian, can't you turn that blasted thing off!" she scowls and then buries her nose into the pillow, clenching it up to her ears in two fists.

"I'm bloody well trying, woman! Please give me a break; I can't reach it!"

"Just pull the bloody plug out of the wall!" Cynthia says in a muffled reply.

Sebastian, now panicking, yanks on the cord and the bedside lamp comes crashing down on his head, "Ow, shit! Shit! Ow shit, shit, shit!" he says, as he sits back on his calves, while rapidly rubbing his head with one hand and holding the lamp in the other.

Cynthia hurtles out of bed like a springbok being pursued by a starving lion and turns off the offending alarm at the plug, snatches the lamp from his hand and puts it back on the bedside table. "Goodness gracious, Sebastian! The one day I get to sleep in and you do this to me. Now can you go and have your shower so I can get back to sleep?"

Sebastian mumbles a few choice words under his breath while pushing the sleep from his right eye with his index finger. After the rough start to his morning, he appreciates the soothing warmth of the water as it gently massages his emotional and physical aches and pains down the drain and he unwillingly departs from his comforting enclosure. Alert and ready for a new day he dresses and moves stealthily downstairs to the kitchen, turns on the percolator and looks at the clock, only to realise he is still ahead of schedule. Sebastian, knowing Cynthia is asleep upstairs; figures one hearty breakfast won't ruin his diet too much. He opens the fridge, stands there smiling for a few seconds and then pulls out two big rashers of bacon, an onion and two eggs. Once the pan is sizzling he pours himself a coffee and sips away as he merrily flips his eggs. The aroma of frying bacon and onions fills the air and he is just about to plate up when the front doorbell chimes.

"Paul, you're early! What's up?" Sebastian says with a concerned look.

"Nothing at all, Seb. I had to drop Chelsea off at the airport so rather than go back home, I thought I'd come here. You don't mind, do you? I can go for a drive if you would rather I come back later."

Sebastian gives a tight-lipped grin. "Actually, I put a little extra breakfast on this morning in case you did call in. Are you hungry?"

"You bet!" Paul bounces into the kitchen like an eager puppy. "Where's Cynthia this morning?"

Sebastian glances up from the frypan as he dishes up the meal. "She is having a well-deserved sleep in."

"Good for her. I don't mean this rudely, Seb, but she looked a little worn the other day," Paul replies sincerely. No sooner the food is on the plate they scoff it down in record time and head for the car.

Paul looks back. "Where's your cane?"

Sebastian stops dead in his tracks and throws his head upwards, "Bugger! No time to go back now; I will just have to leave it today,"

Paul turns his head to one side. "I don't think so, Seb. I was told by Cynthia to make sure you carried it wherever you go. She convinced me it had saved your bacon on more than one occasion. Is that right?"

Sebastian waves his head like an unsettled stallion. "Yes but we are going to a bloody gym! Who in god's good name takes a cane to a bloody gym?"

Paul opens the palms of both hands. "Sorry, Seb, but I would rather face the Commissioner on a disciplinary matter than Cynthia."

Sebastian rolls his eyes upwards – "I see your point!" –So he retrieves his cane and they leave without any further ado.

As they flow over one of the higher hills on the way to the gym, they get a bird's eye view of how the city buildings dwarf and overshadow the rows of trees and shrubs that line the dank streets. Unlike the vivid greens and golds of those that grow on the outskirts of town, they have become pale and discoloured by the dust and exhaust fumes that spew's out of the traffic that hurtles past.

Paul pulls the car across from the gym in an inconspicuous spot and both men don their overcoats upon alighting; it has been a bitter winter and the start of spring sees an array of weather from freezing cold mornings to sunny and wet days and this is one of those days most people would prefer to spend indoors, in front of a warm fire.

The gym sits perfectly placed amongst trendy cafés that line both sides of the street, and Sebastian and Paul enjoy the atmosphere created by the bitterly cold morning and the inviting aroma of freshly brewed coffee which wafts toward them tantalizing their senses. Paul stands for a brief moment with his eyes closed, pushes out his chin and inhales deeply.

Sebastian notices his dreamy expression. "It isn't hard to tell that coffee is a source of infinite delight to you, Paul," Sebastian groans sarcastically.

"You better believe it, Seb! How did people ever survive without it?" he replies with little interest in how Sebastian perceives his overwhelming enjoyment.

Sebastian rolls his eyes. "Well I know one thing for sure; they didn't die of bloody pneumonia! Now are you going to lock the car so I can go into the gym before I catch my death?"

"Ah, no. Actually I'm not. It seems to me that you may have left something lying across the rear seat. Oh, what do you know? It looks like your cane!"

Sebastian sends a heavy mist billowing from his mouth. "For goodness sakes, man, we have already left the house and Cynthia will see it's not in the hallstand, so what she doesn't know won't hurt her!"

Paul grimaces. "Sorry Seb. She might not know but I gave her my word. You wouldn't want me to go back on my word now, would you? I mean, you are old enough to make your own decisions and I can't force you into taking it but I would have to let Cynthia know."

Sebastian seethes and his eyes bounce rapidly from one side to the other in frustration. After a defiant moment, he lets out another gust of mist, opens the rear door and snatches his cane from the seat. "Great! I'm taking a bloody cane into a gym, how very novel of me. And to top it off, I now have a bloody giant nursemaid who is under instructions from my wife!"

Paul smiles warmly. "Thanks, Seb, I do appreciate it. Now if you just take in a whiff of that wonderful aroma, you will feel so much better." He gracefully waves his right hand toward Seb's nose.

"Well, I can't imagine what you will be doing while I'm in humiliating myself at the gym. Oh, wait a minute! I think I have just had a bolt from the blue! Correct me if I'm wrong but you are about to partake in a hot cup of coffee? And with any luck, it'll burn your lips so bad they will swell up and look like the rear end of a baboon!"

Paul ignores his sarcasm. "More than coffee!" he replies gleefully.

Sebastian looks angrily where Paul is pointing at a sign that reads, '9AM TO 10 AM BUFFET BREAKFAST & BOTTOMLESS COFFEE $10.00 TODAY ONLY'. He turns, his brow folded and eyes squinted. "What the heck is up with you, man? Have you got worms?"

Unperturbed, Paul grins. "Gotta do something while you're in there... and look at the price! When are you going to get a deal like that again?"

Sebastian throws his eyes to the sky and storms toward the gym. As his feet hit the pavement on the far side of the road, he hears cooing but can't work out where it's coming from until he reaches a narrow alleyway next to the gym; a flock of a dozen or so pigeons startle Sebastian by wheeling in the early morning silence, wings flapping. An eerie buzzing sound fades as they take to the air for the ledges that protrude from higher buildings. Sebastian looks back to see if Paul had seen him shy in shock but he's already halfway to his ten dollar breakfast. No one else is in sight; he takes a deep breath and continues on his way.

It has been years since Sebastian has visited any type of fitness or training facility, and even then by invitation from the Olympic Coach, so he looks more than a little awkward with his coat bunched in one hand and a walking stick, in the other. Just to top it off, a jacket and tie aren't exactly perfect gym attire either. Small details like these never really deter Sebastian as his thoughts are solidly focused on the job at hand. Even though he has mellowed and has become a little less self-conscious in recent times, his early, embedded beliefs still linger. His issue with the cane is more about being told what he must do rather than how he looks. How others perceive him is irrelevant; he contemplates such thinking as shallow conceptions of an idle mind; his own head is so occupied with other things there's no room for what he sees as wasted thoughts.

Sebastian is surprised by the enormity of the interior. The receptionist sit sat a semi-circular desk directly across from the entrance and to the right and left, small booths sell gym equipment, health food and sports drinks. He informs the receptionist that he has an appointment with the manager, Max

Martin and she rings through to his office at the rear of the building and then points Sebastian in that direction.

The path to his office leads Sebastian directly through the workout area and his senses fill with an overpowering smell of liniment, the sound of clanging metal and muffled voices of patrons and instructors. He eyes everything around him in a desultory manner, as he strives to familiarise himself with the scene.

Only a few strides along, there is disharmony between a middle-aged pair. She is trying to encourage her partner to stay close and he is making it overtly obvious that he's there against his will. Sebastian slows his pace and continues to observe them.

He will often challenge himself to understand what others communicate with their bodies rather than orally and walking through the gym gives him an opportunity to hone his already exceptional skills. The woman constantly pulls at her jacket in an attempt to prevent it creeping upward means she is carrying more weight than she would like. As the fellow is quite muscular and lean, Sebastian muses, she may have dragged him along because of her own insecurities. She flutters from one machine to the next in her matching pink tracksuit and joggers like a bee in floral heaven. In contrast, her partner's outfit – camouflaged cargo pants and sleeveless checked shirt – isn't your regular gym attire but that of a woodsman, hunter or labourer.

Sebastian is soon bored with these two. Spying a spritely young woman about to board a treadmill, his mood soon changes to one of being inspired, as he ponders the thought of buying one for home. He murmurs to himself, "Mmm. That would certainly save me being late to breakfast again!"

Now Sebastian comes across the 'real deal'; one rather solidly built fellow lies flat on a slab and above him sits a set of gigantic weights, held together with a bar surely way too lean for the enormous discs it supports. A muscular friend, or perhaps trainer, is arched over, ready to take the torturous weight from its racks and lower the bar carefully down. There's no doubt in Sebastian's mind that these two are gym enthusiasts, disciplined and dedicated, something that he admires, even if he has no interest in the activity.

On he goes until his eyes abruptly shift to the right. "Well, well, well, there's hope for me yet!" he exclaims as he catches sight of a massive form of a man trying to keep rhythm with his overlapping stomach on yet another treadmill. Sebastian is so enthralled he doesn't see a rather plump, middle-aged woman cross his path. As they collide, his hand flies out and accidently grabs hold of her ample breast. "Sorry, sorry!"

She stands there smiling at him, glances down at the hand that has yet to disconnect from her bosom. Sebastian also glances down then back up. His mouth opens; his forehead wrinkles and he gives an involuntary smile before releasing the object like a red hot ember. To make matters worse he's so flustered he begins brushing down her breast in a reflex action.

"It's fine. You can stop now". She says smiling warmly and gently nodding her head.

Sebastian hesitantly smiles back and then leaves as quickly as he can, no longer interested in anything except his destination.

After a long loping stroll at a good pace, he finally reaches the manager's office. An immaculately dressed and powerfully built man sits behind a modern desk strewn with paperwork and bodybuilding magazines. His hairline is receding and his tight, light blue, Italian shirt bulges from the muscular outcrops that lay beneath. The strong but pleasant smell of cologne wafts through the office.

"Max Martin and you must be Mr Cork. How can I help you?" he says in a deep gruff voice that can only be compared to a heavyweight wrestler.

Sebastian hesitantly steps forward, preparing himself for a bone crushing grip, but this mountain man's grip is firm but gentle.

"Nice to meet you, Max but please call me Seb as you know..."

Max interrupts "Before you continue, Seb, let me get you a seat." He reaches around the corner and pulls a plastic scoop chair into the office. "There you go. Is there anything else I can get you?"

"No, I'm fine. Thank you very much."

They both take a seat. "As I was saying," Sebastian continues, "I am here to investigate the murder of Michael Cohen. I have spoken to my superior and it is okay to inform staff and other people who knew Michael that he is deceased; it won't be long before it makes the papers anyway. Can you tell me something about him?"

Max sits back in his chair and drops his head to one side. "I didn't have too much to do with him. What is it exactly you want to know?"

Sebastian places his elbows on Max's desk and folds a fist inside the palm of his other hand. "Well, for a start, what was your perception of his personality?"

Max slumps back and crosses his arms. "In all honesty, Sebastian, I don't like to speak ill of the dead – or anyone for that matter–but I have met a lot of elite athletes during my time and am aware of how focused they are, so I try to ensure they are left alone. But Michael came into the gym as cocky as a new rooster in a pen full of hens and started demanding this and that."

"So how did you handle that Max?"

Max's eyes widen and his lips tighten. "It wasn't easy. On one hand we didn't want to lose him because someone of his status will always bring us additional clientele. I mean, when friends mention that a well-known athlete attends their gym... well, you know what I mean. But on the other hand, no matter how high and mighty an athlete thinks they are, there is only so much pampering you can do before the other clients feel they're being treated second rate. So it becomes a matter of balance."

Sebastian leans back and places his hands flat on the desk. "As much as I hate to ask this..."

"I know what you are about to ask," Max interrupts. "I've been working seven days a week for the last five years to make this business a success. Once it began to do well I decided to take my wife somewhere she had always wanted to go, so up until two days ago we have been touring China." Max pulls his passport from his top drawer and shows Sebastian, "I brought this with me today because I thought this question might come up."

Sebastian relaxes into the chair. "Thank you for being so candid, I appreciate it. Now I have a big favour to ask of you."

"Go ahead; I'm only too happy to help."

Sebastian bites his bottom lip as his eyes bounce to and fro "Well, we would like one of our detectives to join the gym and you would be the only person who would know he is undercover. Could you work with that?"

Max nods in the affirmative, "I don't have a problem with that at all but what will you need me to do?

Sebastian opens his hands and curls one corner of his mouth, "Nothing we just wanted to inform you of our plans, that's all and if you see or remember anything of interest to us; we would like to be informed immediately. Here is my card."

"I can do that."

"Good. Now that is all sorted, I have a few questions regarding certain people who have frequented the gym recently."

Max nods again.

"Can you tell me something about Nathan Spedding?"

"Yes. Nathan was a hell of a nice guy. I don't think he would have spent as much time trying to push his advertising if it wasn't for Kate." Sebastian screws up the corner of his mouth while rapidly shaking his head. "Sorry, Sebastian, that was stupid of me. There's no way known you'd know who Kate is. She has a shop that sells power drinks within the complex. Nathan seemed to have a strong interest in her."

Sebastian tilts his head slightly, "How do you mean?"

Max's eyes seek the ceiling as he ponders his answer. "Well, not in the romantic sense, more of an interest in her background. He was always asking me if I knew anything about her family. Of course I told him no, as I don't." Max shuffles a magazine around his desk. "Do you think Nathan had something to do with Mike's murder?"

Sebastian sits back in the seat. "So you don't know?" he leans forward again in a serious manner. "Before I explain some things to you, I need you to understand that what I'm about to tell you is highly confidential."

This time Max leans forward and crosses his forearms on the desk. "Of course, of course," he replies with curious concern.

Sebastian scratches his head, indecisive about how much to reveal. "Nathan had nothing to do with Mike's murder; in fact he was killed in a similar fashion."

Max's eyes open wide with astonishment, which confirms to Sebastian that he has had nothing to do with either murder. Finally, he gains his composure, "So are you saying that the murderer... no, a **serial killer** could be walking amongst my patrons?"

Sebastian remembers Jim's concerns about public disclosure. "A serial killer? No I doubt it, but a possible connection. That's why we want one of our men in here, to keep a close eye on things."

Max rubs his pitch-black receding hair, and then looks at Sebastian accusingly. "Are you sure this nut case, that may or may not be running loose in my gym, isn't a serial killer; I don't want to put my people at risk!"

Sebastian knows he has to dispel Max's thoughts regarding a serial killer so he gently nods his head and explains, "I understand your trepidation, Max, but as a psychologist I can tell you many serial killers will commit their murders within a few miles of each other. They will also kill numerous victims in the same place at the same time, but they rarely revisit a public place where they have murdered before." Sebastian knows only too well that the murders haven't taken place in the gym as the victims have been murdered elsewhere.

"Okay, so what's next?" Max asks in a warmer tone.

Sebastian keeps the conversation rolling to distract any further thoughts of a serial killer; he doesn't dare tell Max about Owen Coleman as he knows this would surely put the cat amongst the pigeons.

"Was there anyone one else connected with Kate who seemed suspicious to you?"

Max puckers his mouth to one side in thought and replies, "Only one guy. His name was Owen... yes, that's right, Owen Coleman, but that's going back a bit. I never liked him at all."

Sebastian is keen to get more information and responds quickly, "Really? Why is that?"

"He just came across as sleazy, that's all. I mean Kate really had feelings for that guy. He'd take her out for lunch and everyone could see that they had a thing going on. Right up until she found out the guy was married; that's when she dumped him like a hot potato."

"Worst thing was, it really broke her heart and I believe she never got over it. As for him, he just disappeared from the scene; if he hadn't I would have kicked him the hell out anyway. I don't normally interfere but Kate's a bit of a loner and people here are like family, so we tend to look after our own. Anyway, apart from him, I haven't noticed any others that seem suspicious and as I said, that was quite awhile ago."

Sebastian decides at this point he should veer the conversation away from Owen Coleman. "Is there anyone else you can think of that may have some idiosyncrasies that prevent them fitting in, or have had confrontations at the gym?" Max screws his nose up and Sebastian, always the observer, is quick to jump, "Come on, Max! Who are you protecting?"

Max cocks his head back. "What do you mean?"

"When I spoke of confrontation your lips tightened, pushing your cheeks upward. Someone came to mind when the word 'confrontation' was used and now the frown that brings your eyebrows together tells me I'm right."

"What are you, some sort of expert in facial expressions?"

"Something like that but that's not important. Who are you protecting?"

Max looks to the ceiling. "I'm not really protecting anyone - well, not in the sense that I think they have committed a murder and I'm trying to keep that from you - but Jamie Hanigan, who is my best personal trainer and runs the social club here, did have an altercation with Mike a few weeks ago. I was hoping you wouldn't ask me that question; I was sure you'd get the wrong idea and start jumping to conclusions."

Sebastian sits back again, "In all reality, Max, you don't know me and you could well be jumping to conclusions by assuming that."

"Fair call. Look, Jamie's been with me for six years and the only complaint that's been lodged against him came from Mike Cohen. Mike detested homosexuality; he had upset a couple female patrons with name-calling prior his confrontation with Jamie."

"So, Jamie is gay?" Sebastian paraphrases.

"Hell, yes, everyone in the gym knows that! Anyway, Jamie tried to point out to Mike that he wasn't lifting a weight correctly and he made some pretty insulting remarks about Jamie being gay. He tried to walk away from a confrontation but Mike threw a full bottle of water at him, hitting him in the back of the head. Jamie was furious, as anyone would be, so he turned around and grabbed Mike by the throat. A couple of the other clients noticed what was going on and got in between them. Immediately after the confrontation, Mike comes to me with a complaint. I called Jamie into the office and let him know I wouldn't tolerate that sort of loss of control from my staff. He understood he'd done the wrong thing so he apologised to Mike. Mike told me he wanted Jamie fired or he would press charges for assault but I told him that wasn't going to happen. I had witnesses who saw him assault Jamie first so he backed off. Mike realised that it wouldn't look good for him with his sponsors if the truth came out. The one thing he did do though was demand another personal trainer and we were only too happy to accommodate him. There were no more problems. Now, I know that sounds bad for Jamie but he would never have killed him; he's not like that."

Sebastian pulls at his chin with his right hand. "Did you write a report on the incident?"

"Yes, but as I said, I don't believe Jamie would ever kill anyone."

Sebastian, still in thought, ignores Max's statement. "Is there any chance of getting a copy of your report for my own file?"

Max rolls his desk chair back, retrieves a file from the metal cabinet and places it on the photocopier. Once done, he hands Sebastian the copy and places the rest back in the cabinet.

Sebastian scans through it and looks over to Max who has his hands behind his head in frustration. "I'm sorry to pry, Max, but it's important I ask these questions. Do you know where he worked before coming here?"

Max hesitates to answer and then responds reluctantly. "Jamie had been in prison. He was finding it hard to get a job so his parole officer gave me a call and asked if we had any positions available. Don't ask me what Jamie had done as I didn't want to know unless it had something to do with hurting kids. The parole officer told me it was nothing to do with that, so I hired him."

Sebastian scratches the middle of his forehead. "Isn't it a bit unusual for a parole officer to ring a gym on behalf of a client?"

"Not in this case. The officer was a long time member here until he couldn't fit it into his hectic schedule anymore. Look, I know this doesn't look good for Jamie but, honestly, Sebastian he really is a great guy and is loved by both the staff and clients. I'd go as far to say that without a doubt I would trust him with my life."

Max is feeling uncomfortable and defensive and Sebastian doesn't want to make an enemy of him so he's quick to move on, "Look, Max, everyone has their issues, so let's get off Jamie for now and perhaps you can think of another member of staff that's a bit of a misfit?"

Max hits the tips of his fingers on his desk. "Of course! Joe Devonport, I don't know why I didn't think of him earlier," he replies while tossing his eyes upward at his thoughtlessness.

"Tell me about this Joe Devonport; is he a customer or a worker here?"

"Joe's all that and a bit more. He has a delivery business and he does deliveries for Kate but for a while there his business wasn't doing so well, so we gave him some work around the gym as the odd jobs man. He's on his feet now but I'd like to keep him on staff as he's a diligent worker. He's a small fellow and although he doesn't look it, he's very strong as he works out in his free time. Joe has access to everything in the gym and has a bit of a chip on his shoulder when it comes to taller guys but we just see him as a bit of a character. That's why he didn't come to mind."

This statement piques Sebastian's attention. "How did he get on with Michael Cohen?"

Max pauses and thinks for a moment. "As strange as this sounds, he seemed to get along better with Mike than most others."

"Really, how so?"

"Well it was rare for Mike to give anyone the time of day but when it came to Kate and Joe, they all got along quite well. Then again, Joe and Mike seemed to be a bit distant just before Mike disappeared."

Sebastian grasps his bottom lip in his fingertips and then probes further, "Did anyone witness an argument between them?"

"No, nothing like that; the water just ran cold, that's all."

Sebastian pushes down on his cane and rises to his feet. "Well, I would like to thank you so much for your time and patience, Max. Now I really must leave you to do your work and also get back to mine. Hopefully we will meet again under more favourable circumstances."

Max leans across the desk and shakes his hand. "Before you go, Sebastian, would like to have a tour of the gym? We do cater for mature people as well, you know."

"Well, I am starting to run out of time."

Max smiles. "Come on. Fifteen minutes, that's all it will take. I'm sure you can spare a measly fifteen minutes."

Sebastian gives this proposition bona fide consideration and assents. Before his tour with Max, he jots down names and events and then excuses himself to make a quick phone call to Paul, so he knows how long he has to finish whatever it is he is doing.

Max and Sebastian leisurely stroll through another wing of the gym that he has yet to see and Sebastian is enthralled by the latest edition of treadmills.

"Tell me, Max, is it possible for someone like myself to purchase one of those?"

"No, not normally, Sebastian, but I could purchase one for you if you like."

Sebastian turns to Max excitedly, "Let me think about it, Max. I would probably have to build a home gym first and before I can do that I will need to run it past my beautiful wife."

Sebastian turns to look back at the treadmills. He crashes into the same woman he ran into on the way in and when he realises who it is, his face flushes red.

"Hello again! If you really want to get to know me, all you have to do is ask me for my number and I will give it to you," she says with a sensual grin on her face.

Sebastian's head quickly drops like a naughty child and he looks from one shoe to another in an effort to avoid eye contact, "Ah, no...that's... uh... fine. I mean I'm fine...sorry" Sebastian slowly raises his apprehensive head until his reluctant eyes meet hers.

"Okay, ta, ta for now. But if you change your mind..."

Sebastian looks straight back down at his shoes. "Yes, yes, quite so but I don't think so...but thank you, anyway." He rubs the top of his bowed head with the fingertips of his left hand, making sure his wedding band is in view.

Max puts his hand on Sebastian's shoulder. "Are you alright?"

"Um...yes, I'm fine. Has she gone yet?"

Max squints at him curiously, as he has yet to raise his head. "Yes, she's gone; are you sure you are alright?"

Sebastian straightens and looks around in every possible direction. "Truly, I'm fine. Look, I really must get back to my partner." Max stands there tugging his ear while peering through half-shut eyes as Sebastian scurries toward the exit.

++++

Sebastian puts his jacket on before leaving. He knows he is about to experience an extreme change of temperature and once outside the freezing cold air bites at his face. The one positive factor of these arctic gusts is, the relief it brings to the ruby red heat of his embarrassed cheeks. He shivers in the icy winds as he draws closer to the car and once he has crossed the road he can see Paul sipping on a hot brew. Sebastian desperately hopes Paul has been considerate enough to have bought one for him, as he couldn't think of anything better to ease the uncomforting thoughts of the woman in the gym, than the sensation of sitting in the heated vehicle sipping on a warm coffee.

He quickly bundles himself into the waiting sedan with eager anticipation. "Bloody freezing out there!" he over emphasises and begins blowing into his cupped hands.

Paul takes another sip from his disposable cup. "I know, right? I'm really glad you give me fifteen minutes warning; it allowed me time to grab another cup of coffee. I always think it tastes better in this climate, don't you?"

Sebastian glares disconcertingly. "I wouldn't know, Paul, I haven't got one; have I!"

Paul glances over at Sebastian in a nonchalant manner. "No but I'm sure you have experienced a warm coffee on a cold day; haven't you?"

Sebastian sighs deeply, "whatever Paul can we get back to the office please!" he declares sternly and then turns to look out his window.

Paul grins. "A bit grumpy, are we?"

Still looking out the window Sebastian insists, "Paul, Can we just get back please!"

Paul opens his door and begins to get out of the car.

Sebastian's first reaction is a semi-turn of the head, then a hard jerk around when the cold outside air hits him. "Where the hell are you going, Paul?"

Paul pokes his head back in. "Just getting my jacket, Seb, I'm still a little cold."

Sebastian's eyes bulge from his head. "Well you wouldn't be if you kept the bloody car door shut!" Paul just smiles, pulls his head back out and goes to the rear door. "For goodness sake, how much more can a mere mortal bear?"

"Aha! That's where you're hiding, you sneaky little devil!" Sebastian swings his body around to berate Paul but he smiles from the back seat and holds another cup of coffee toward him. "There you go, Seb. You didn't really think I would let you go without one, did you?"

Sebastian smiles, as he swings his head from side to side. "Thank you, my friend. I really appreciate your thoughtfulness, even if it does come with a price."

Paul settles back into the driver's seat, starts the motor and moves out into traffic

Sebastian takes a sip and makes a clicking noise with his mouth like a dog licking water, "Where did you have it hidden?"

Paul glances over, "under my jacket Seb."

Sebastian frowns and begins poking his tongue out over his lips while pulling a strange face, "that's unhealthy you know. I don't think I can drink this!"

Paul has his eyes fixed on the slippery road ahead but a large frown appears on his forehead when he hears the passenger window going down, "What the hell!" He swings his head rapidly toward Sebastian; only to find him with a childish grin on his face. "You bastard Seb, I honestly thought you were going to throw it out the window! Sebastian's smile broadens further.

"Why would I do that?" Anyway, you should know by now I'm not one who likes to play mind games," he jokes and then follows up with a long sip of his coffee.

Paul sets his eyes back on the road but can't stop from smiling all the way back to the office.

++++

Sebastian likes to keep some parts of investigations to himself. He believes others may jump to conclusions before he has had the opportunity to follow all his own suspicions.

Soon as they arrive back at the Station he heads for the Dust Pit and rings Cynthia while Paul goes to the shooting range to get some practice in while things are quiet.

"Hi, it's me. I'm wondering if you can do me a favour."

Cynthia is busily setting out invitations for a charity function she and Clarissa will be hosting in a few weeks. "What's the problem, Seb? Is everything alright?" She knows full well Sebastian can get himself into trouble at the drop of a hat.

"No problem at all, my love. I was hoping you can make some calls for me regarding a fellow by the name of Jamie Hanigan. His parole officer is a fellow by the name of Samuel James. Apparently Jamie did some time a good while back and I am hoping you can find out why."

Cynthia makes her way to her office so she can jot down Jamie's name. "Okay, I have that. By the way, where are you now?"

Sebastian hesitates. "I'm in my office, my love, "he grimaces and as he awaits her reply.

A moment's silence.

"Sorry, Seb? I thought I heard you say you are at your office at the station?"

"That **is** where I am but there is a reason..."

Before he can finish his explanation, Cynthia responds angrily, "So let me get this straight... you just rang me from your office **at the station** and interrupted what I was doing so I can ring **the station** to find out about some fellow's jail term. Now tell me, Seb how many officers could have..."

"You haven't given me the opportunity to explain, Cynthia," he jumps in. "I know there are dozens of people down here who can help me, and I also know that when I gave over too much information on the last case, everyone jumped to the conclusion that an innocent man had committed a murder. So there are certain aspects of this case I would like to find out about discreetly. Now, with all due respect, do you know anyone who can get me the information I need without broadcasting it to the world?"

Cynthia tightens her lips so hard her eyes squint and her nose wrinkles. "Sorry Seb I have fallen a bit behind today but that's no excuse for not hearing you out. Anyway, I have an attorney friend who will be able to get the information you need, so I will ring you back after I have spoken to him."

"Thankyou, my love, and perhaps if I had explained my reasons from the beginning, you may not have misunderstood my motives."

An hour passes and Sebastian receives a call back.

"Hi Seb, here's what I have for you. Hanigan was found guilty of attempted murder when he was twenty-one, received a fifteen-year sentence and was released on good behaviour after twelve. Apparently a barman had refused to serve him any more drinks because he was intoxicated and Hanigan lashed out with a broken glass, slicing into his neck and just missing the carotid artery. The judge went light on him because he had no previous record and it was proven that his system had a low tolerance for alcohol. Since then he has had no further issues with the law."

There's a slight pause on Sebastian's end of the phone. "So it wasn't premeditated?"

"Exactly, Seb.Hard to say without further investigation but he doesn't seem to fit the serial profile."

"I have to agree my dear a serial killer is normally much more cautious and rarely acts impulsively in front of a gathering of people. Well thank you, my love; as usual, you have made my job so much easier."

"Oh before you go… that parole officer you asked me to do a follow up on, Samuel Peters? He's recently retired but I have his number and address. Would you like them?"

Sebastian is quick to reply. "Most definitely Cynthia, this is much more than I expected."

Cynthia relates her findings to Sebastian and then leaves him to his afternoon.

Paul arrives back from the range to pick up Sebastian and on the drive home they discuss their plans for the following day.

"So, your big day at the gym tomorrow, Paul. Have you thought out how you are going to approach it?"

Keeping his eyes on the road, Paul replies, "I've worked out at a few gyms, Seb, and patrons normally don't mind you asking a question or two if they think you are new and trying to fit in. I'll just browse around like I'm looking for something and ask where it is and then strike up a conversation."

"I'm impressed, Paul!"

"We were trained in these types of approaches in the Service, where we had to intermingle with town folk incognito," he says proudly.

As usual Sebastian's thoughts are jumping ahead. "If you get a chance, turn your focus to Kate Kensington at some point; her name keeps popping up in conversations and I am curious to know what kind of person she is."

Paul pulls into Sebastian's driveway, where they finish their conversation. "What about you; what are you going to do?"

"I'm going to stay home in the morning to finish up some paperwork then meet you in the office when you have finished at the gym."

They say their farewells and Paul heads out through the gates. Sebastian has a relaxing evening after dinner by the open fire with Cynthia.

Paul arrives at the gym early and begins working his way around the different equipment, while casually chatting with patrons. Halfway through his workout he decides to get himself an energy drink from Kate's Cool It Bar. When he enters he notices the left side of the shop is set out like a saloon and to the right, glass fridges filled with juices. As he looks over all the different flavours in the glass fridges, he doesn't notice Kate slip out from behind the counter but he soon cranks his head around with a start when she says, "Hi I'm Kate, can I help you with anything?"

Paul's taken aback by her glowing blonde hair, striking smile and soft spoken voice. Her face is round without a blemish and she's built more like a small ballroom-dancer than a gym junkie. Kate has no tattoos or even much makeup, and there's nothing novel about her white sweat shirt or faded blue jeans, yet somehow, something about her is pleasant. She could fit in anywhere. There is only one flaw he can see and that is her eyes are lifeless; when she stops smiling, her expression seems stark.

"I'm sorry. Did I startle you?"

"No, not at all... okay, maybe a little." Paul moves quickly to change the subject, so he has time to consider his approach. "Did you develop these drinks yourself?" he asks, suavely.

She beams a smile as she admires his physique, good looks and vivid blue eyes. "Yes. I was a chemist before realizing most things we eat and drink aren't good for us; so this is my way of saying you don't require processed sugar and chemicals to be healthy." She goes to a fridge beneath the long counter which is cleverly shaped like a saloon bar. "What flavour would you like? I give a free sample to first time customers. So, as they say in the movies, what's your poison?"

Paul chuckles and rubs his chin in thought. "Well, let's have a go at the pineapple, plum and gooseberry."

Kate pushes a glass across the counter to him. He looks the concoction up and down with some doubt then takes a long slow gulp. Paul's head springs back sharply and his eyes blink rapidly. "Wow! That has one heck of a kick but it is so refreshing. I'll definitely have a bottle of that. Thanks."

Kate grins with his acknowledgement and then looks at him inquisitively. "Are you new to the gym?"

"Sorry, I should have introduced myself. My name's Paul and yes I am."

Kate washes out the glass in a small sink. "So what brings you to this gym, Paul?"She glances over her shoulder at him.

"Well I have a few months business here in town and I'm a bit of a gym junkie. Listen... I know I'm going to sound a little cheeky. I'm, um, a bit short on time today but I'd like to get to know you better, Kate. The only people I know in town are my business associates and they can be a little boring; so I was wondering if you would, ah, like to join me for a coffee sometime?"

Kate grins nervously, "How do you know you won't find me even more boring?"

Paul opens the palms of his hands, smiles and tilts his head. "There's only one way to find out; how about it?"

Kate sighs, "I can't today," she says. "I have a delivery coming in. How about early tomorrow morning, will that fit in with your schedule?"

"I'll make it fit in!" They make arrangements for the following morning. Paul heads back in to work out for another hour and then showers before leaving for the station.

++++

Sebastian is methodically reading and scanning through the Coroner's reports and photos of the murders prior to Mike Cohen's when Paul enters the Dust Pit. "I've set up a meeting with Kate for tomorrow like you asked. How do you want me to handle it, Seb?"

Sebastian's brow folds as he peers upward while barely moving his head. "And a good afternoon to you too Paul." He puts down the photo he's holding and leans back in his chair. "It's not for me to tell you how to do your job, my friend but I am happy to explain to you how I would approach such a situation. Keep the conversation as general and casual as possible. Use probing questions sparingly but when probing, watch her body gestures like an insect under a microscope. Carry a pen and notebook to make notes immediately after meeting with her." He ticks the points off on his fingers.

Paul takes a seat across the desk. "Wouldn't it be easier to memorise my observations and wait until I get back here so I can tell you verbally? I mean really, Seb. My memory's not that bad!"

Sebastian leans forward in his chair while crossing his arms on the desk and Paul prepares himself for a lecture. "Paul, I understand you don't have a degree in psychology, nor are you a psychoanalyst but I thought you would be trained well enough to know memory not only distorts past events but small important facts can be lost while focusing on major developments. If you really want to do it my way, it is imperative to be two people at once."

"On one hand you maintain a friendly enquiring personality, while on the other, you are a blank canvas. In other words, put aside your detective role and observe all you see and hear. Inhale the information as you would inhale air and keep it as pure as you possibly can, without adding your own interpretation. Above all observe her body movements and gestures for they may indicate more than her actual words."

This is all new to Paul but he knows that Sebastian's methods work and he's keen to learn from him. "Okay, point taken. I'll take notes straight after the meeting with her."

Sebastian sinks back into his chair and looks at Paul as he would at his ex-students. "I understand my methods seem a little complicated at times and I would like to simplify it for you by explaining how I worked in my practice."

"The first visit with a client, I called my observation session. I would simply ask relevant questions while observing the client's reactions. There would be no assessments made during the interview. I would then take notes immediately afterwards: whether the client swallows, blushes, pulls at the collar of their shirt, crosses their arms or just maintains silence."

"The following visit I called the probing session; this would be like a gentle interrogation of those things that made them uncomfortable during the previous interview. Does that make sense to you, Paul?"

Paul nods and begins taking notes.

As investigators we may only get one interview, so we combine the two while always remaining aware to ease up if the interviewee is getting uncomfortable with the questioning, thus preventing withdrawal of other information.

Paul continues to jot down his notes while Sebastian decides to focus on Kate as well and rings Cynthia for some help.

"Hello, my love. How has your day been?"

"Hi Seb, it has been unusually quiet. I had plans to see Clarissa for lunch but she's come down with a nasty bug."

"I'm so sorry to hear that," Sebastian says as he musters a little sympathy. "Well, hopefully, I can fill in some of your day with a small chore."

"Yes Sebastian, what is it?" she hisses while paying umbrage to his lack of empathy for her friend.

"Oh good, I'm glad I can help do something about your boredom. I wonder if you can run a background on Kate Kensington. She runs her own sports energy drink store at the gym."

"My **goodness**, Sebastian, do you **ever** listen to your own words before you make a statement?"

Sebastian goes quiet for a moment. "How can I possibly listen to my own words before making a statement? Do you mean, do I ever think about what I am about to say before I say it? Well the answer, of course, is yes. Why?"

There's silence as Cynthia's chin hits her chest and her arms drop limply by her side. Then she angrily brings the phone back up to her ear and barks, "I will see what I can do. Goodbye, Sebastian!" Before he can reply, the phone goes dead.

Sebastian's eyes bounce around momentarily and then he makes one more call and focuses his attention back to Paul, "I have just made an appointment tomorrow to meet up with a guy by the name of Samuel James. I should be starting my meeting just as you are finishing yours and I will meet you back here later to exchange notes."

Paul looks up from his writing. "Who's he?"

"Look, Paul, I hope I can trust you to keep this hush hush. Can you do that for me please?"

"I would be a liar if I told you that without knowing the facts but if I don't feel you will be placing yourself in danger or breaking the rules, I will give you my word."

Sebastian nods in agreement. "Samuel James was Jamie Hanigan's old parole officer; apparently Jamie served time awhile back and I want to get a better understanding of whether or not he is capable of these murders. There are a couple of reasons why I would like to keep this quiet. First, I don't want Jim or anyone else on the force jumping to conclusions before he is thoroughly investigated. Second, there's a strong possibility he has been on the straight and narrow for some time and if people got word of what he did in his past he may lose his momentum to remain a model citizen."

"What did he do Seb? It sounds fairly serious."

Sebastian goes on to tell Paul the reason why Jamie Hanigan was charged and Paul listens intently."I can see why you don't want to let this cat out of the bag! Anyway, you have my word and good luck with the interview."

Sebastian semi-smiles and begins putting his paperwork into one pile and then packing it away into a lockable draw. "It's been a long, drawn out day, Paul, and I have had enough. I am going home to my wife and a cold glass of bourbon on the rocks. I will see you tomorrow afternoon."

Paul smiles broadly, "Perhaps I should become a consultant and work my own hours like you do. What a great life!"

Sebastian grins, "Perhaps one day you will. But for now, work hard and continue to visualize where you want to be and the steps required to get there. Good afternoon my friend."

The morning is crisp and Paul feels a bitter chill as he steps out of his car. He takes his black woollen jacket from the rear seat and as he strolls down the road toward the coffee shop, he notices pigeons weaving boldly in and out from under the empty cast iron tables that line the pavement outside the variety of eateries and cafés. They are not intimidated by the giants who stride past above them. Unrelenting in their search for food, their heads bob back and forth intently, scanning for any morsel they can find.

Although it's early, there is a constant flow of traffic shooting clouds of mist from exhaust pipes. The blast of a horn further up the road, where vehicles are beginning to bank up, loses its clarity amongst the sounds of the city's newborn day.

The redolence of freshly brewed coffee intermingles with other culinary delights but it's the distinctive fragrance of caffeine that overrides all other aromas and it continues to grow stronger as Paul draws closer to his destination. On reaching the French doors to the café, he is enchanted by the dew on the small glass windows that gleam like marcasites when the light from the sun momentarily breaks through the clouds and collides with the minute droplets of water.

Paul spies Kate heading his way.

Even though it's become overcast again, Kate's short blond hair glistens like a golden thread caught in a moonbeam. Her neck and shoulders are straight and square while her torso curves nicely. She walks towards him and he notices how light she is on her feet. The Mohair pullover and matching gloves she wears are still penetrable by the morning's cold air and as she reaches Paul, she crosses her arms and shrugs her shoulders, "Oh my goodness, that wind has a bite to it!"

Paul's pushing toward his midriff with his hands in his in his jacket pockets, as he makes every effort to ensure that no drafts permeate his inner sanctum of warmth. With his shoulders pushed high he smiles courteously and replies, "My mother calls it a lazy wind."

Kate looks at him curiously. "Why's that?"

"She says it's too lazy to go around, so it blows straight through you."

Her red cheeks curve upward. Paul pulls one hand from his pocket and gestures the door. "Shall we?" She glides past him and into the warmth of the shop.

"This is so much cosier; I thought I was going to freeze to death out there!" she says while removing her gloves.

"How do you like your coffee?"

"Just a latte for me, please." Paul orders and they work their way through crowded tables where drifts of quiet conversations waft through the warm room, "Look Paul, over there?" Kate points to a quiet corner by the window.

Opposite them sits an unusual, yet closely knit couple: a small balding man with a tufted head with a much taller and thicker set woman, sipping joyfully on their mochas and engage in animated conversation. Many of the executives from surrounding blocks come to this quaint little street where massive buildings loom tall on both sides. They use it as a social hub and hideaway from day to day pressures.

The interior is a mismatch of solid timber tables with comfortable leather and vinyl chairs. The old red brick and white mortar walls make the perfect support for the extremely large oil paintings that hang like window frames throughout the dining area. The buzz of the never ending traffic is muffled from within by the dulcet sounds of pipe music; quietly spoken voices and the intermittent hissing of an espresso machine as the Baristas work their magic. The waitress arrives with their coffees and Paul takes a long sip and smiles with contentment. Kate has been intrigued by him from the moment they met and she can't help but stargaze across the table into his vivid blue eyes.

"What do you do when you're not at the gym, Paul?"

He pauses deliberately and places his cup back on its saucer, "it's pretty boring, really. I'm a property developer. It wasn't what I saw as my ideal career but I'm an only child and when my father retired, I was it." Kate gives him a motherly smile.

"That's not boring at all! In fact, I would imagine it to be quite overwhelming at times."

"Yes, I guess. But it's still a long way from being a football star or a champion athlete."

Her smile turns to disdain. "There have been plenty of sports stars come through the gym and, trust me; they're not all they're cracked up to be." Paul squints and tilts his head to one side.

"How do you mean?"

Kate withdraws as if she's said too much. "Oh, you know... just an ego thing."

Paul's a fast learner and the short time he's been with Sebastian has taught him not to keep pushing. "What about you, Kate? Did you follow in your parents' footsteps with the shop or is this something you wanted to do?"

She hesitates before answering, "No, purely something I wanted to do. I don't have any family; both my parents have passed. My father drowned when I was fourteen and my mother died of cancer when I was nineteen" Paul quickly raises his palms.

"I'm sorry Kate. I shouldn't have asked."

She closes her eyes and smiles warmly, "It's okay Paul, my life is a busy one and I rarely have time to reflect. It may seem callous but I prefer it that way."

He looks sympathetically at her. "I fully understand where you're coming from. In fact that's why I came to the gym in the first place; it keeps me busy and gives me an escape from a career I don't particularly care for. Surely an attractive woman like you has someone special, though?"

"No, no one," she looks at him flirtatiously. "Why do you ask?"

Paul lowers his eyes demurely and he shrugs his shoulders in an effort to downplay the situation. He turns his head to watch people scurry past in an effort to get out of the cold. Kate can see he's feeling uncomfortable. "It's okay, Paul. It's like I said, I don't have much free time in my life."

She takes a mouthful of coffee, "In fact, as much as I'm enjoying our chat, I will have to get back soon."

Paul tries to regain some ground. "Do you ever take a break from it all?"

One corner of her mouth hooks upward in a nonchalant manner. "Oh, sometimes I travel overseas when the urge takes me." Kate's fingers begin nervously tapping. Her brow creases when she sees him staring down at them and she hurriedly throws down the last of her coffee, "I'm sorry Paul; I really do need to get back." They both go to rise at the same time but she holds out her palm. "Please, don't get up. Stay in the warm and finish your coffee. And thank you; I really hope we can do it again soon."

"Most definitely, Kate; I'd love to."

He watches her through the window as she scurries up the street to her car and then he reaches around the back of his chair where his jacket remains limply suspended and pulls out his pen and notebook. He remembers Sebastian's emphasis on making sure he writes only what he sees and not to add his own assumptions; so he quickly scribes the vital points of the conversation, including Kate's facial expressions and body movements and he makes sure he does this while it remains fresh in his mind. After he is finished, he starts motoring his way back to the station.

++++

Sebastian looks at his watch and realises he needs to get a move on for his downtown meeting with Samuel James, so he grabs his coat and cane, checks out with Emily and heads out into the busy street.

The exceptionally cold weather has caused heavy traffic. People don't want to travel on cold public transport and the road is slippery and dangerous, so he feels he will be safer taking a cab. Sebastian works his way through the public, who march up and down the street like ants before the rain. He eventually takes his spot by the curb where he has arranged to be picked up and places one hand in his coat pocket while the other holds his cane. "Where the hell has that bloody driver got to!" he says impatiently aloud, as he lifts his cane up to glare down at his watch as if it's the cause of his problems. A young woman passing by, glances sideways, and pulls away fearfully, thinking he's a mad man.

A horn toots, "HEY! Are you CORK?"

On the other side of the street, a middle-aged man with straggly hair peeking from beneath a navy blue cap yells from the window of his Taxi, Sebastian stands there staring furiously with his mouth agape.

A disdainful glare is well focused. "WELL? Are you CORK or NOT?"

Sebastian's mouth closes and his head cocks back, exposing his double chin, "Well, of COURSE I'm CORK, you bloody FOOL. The only OTHER idiot that would stand out here in this FREEZING COLD is Frosty the Bloody SNOWMAN! What the HELL are you doing over THERE?"

The cabby looks skyward then points forward, "WELL, FROSTY? THIS IS THE DIRECTION WE ARE GOING IN. SO ARE YOU READY OR NOT?"

Sebastian hears murmurs and muffled laughter from the crowd who have gathered behind him; they're all totally immersed in the conversation he is having with the driver. He turns and opens his hands. "Well, what the bloody hell are you all staring at? I should have put a hat down but I don't have a bloody busker's licence!" The group look at each and remain stationary.

Sebastian's head pops forward, "Well!" Just as the crowd are about to move on.

"Hey, FROSTY! The meter's running. Are you COMING or NOT. I have my regular customers, you know?"

Sebastian's lips tighten and his knuckles turn white from clutching the top of his cane. "Yes and they're probably all deaf by now," he mutters under his breath and then begins weaving his way across the busy road. Sebastian almost jumps out of his skin every time someone hits their horn to warn him how close they are and when he finally arrives, shaken but safely on the other side of the road, he hears applause from behind him; apparently, the crowd has been highly entertained.

Beyond furious, he throws himself down on the rear seat of the cab and slams the door.

"Hey! Watch the DOOR, Frosty; you almost took it off its HINGES!"

Sebastian is in sulk mode, stares hypnotically out the window and doesn't utter a word until the driver pulls up outside the unit that belongs to Samuel James. He pays the exact amount for the trip.

"Hey, how about a tip?"

Sebastian turns indignantly. "What?"

The driver holds his hand outstretched from his window. "A tip! What about a tip?"

Sebastian smirks and nods his head in the affirmative. "Yes. Why not? Be GOOD to your MOTHER"

"My mother's dead, Mister Smart Mouth!"

Sebastian turns and walks away. "Then perhaps you should have requested a tip of me a little earlier."

The driver ploughs his foot down and screeches off up the street.

"My God, what is this world coming to? No bloody respect..." Sebastian continues mumbling all the way up to the glass doors of the high-rise. "Hmmm, these apartments seem overly elite for someone who has just retired from being a parole officer." He presses the keypad to announce his arrival.

A slender, fair, middle-aged man meets him at the eighth floor doorway. "Hi there, you must be Mr Cork. How was the traffic?" he says softly with a slight lisp."

Sebastian shakes his hand. "Nice to meet you, Mr James, and please call me Sebastian."

"Only if you call me Sam; please come in."

The living room is well appointed with trinkets from across the globe that would put any luxury suite to shame. An aromatic aroma fills the air from an incense burner and the sound of the rainforest plays low throughout the room.

"Take a seat Sebastian and please excuse the mess. Would you like something to drink?" He says while puffing up one of the cushions on the sofa.

Sebastian sinks back into the plump leather seat, "No. Not for me, thanks. I can't see what mess you are talking about; this place is immaculate. I don't know about your wife but I have no idea how mine does all the things she does and still keeps the home spotless."

Samuel smiles, "I don't have a wife, Sebastian, but I do have a boyfriend who gives me a helping hand whenever he's in town. Being an air steward keeps him away from me for long stints and I do miss his company but, as you can see, he brings me back some wonderful trinkets. Now, before I lose my train of thought, I do have some Earl Grey, so would you like a cup of tea?"

Sebastian is still raspy from all the yelling he did earlier. "I would love an Earl Grey, thank you."

Samuel slips out into the kitchen and a short time later, returns with tea and cake. "There you are. I hope you like carrot cake? I baked it myself."

Sebastian takes a sip and has a nibble, "This is as good as I have tasted, thank you. Sam, I hope you don't mind me saying but, when I heard you had retired from being a parole officer, I imagined you to be a lot older."

Samuel takes his cup and saucer from the small coffee table beside his seat and crosses his legs elegantly. "In all honesty, Sebastian, I never really had to work in the first place. When my parents died in a light plane crash, I was an only child and I was left quite wealthy. The other thing people don't know about me is I write under the pen name of Peter Karston. Perhaps you have heard of the name before?"

Sebastian places his cup back in its saucer and flops back into his seat, "Of course. What an absolute honour! I have read all of your books and, recently, I saw an article by Jacqueline Francis who says you are one of the greatest murder mystery writers of the modern time. We all know Jacqueline is an exceptionally tough critic, so coming from her that is rather special!"

Samuel takes another sip of his tea. "Yes, I read that article as well. Funny how people change; I remember when I wrote my first few books and that bitch called my work naive and lacking substance." Samuel begins to chuckle and Sebastian looks at him curiously. "Sorry, Sebastian I'm just having a giggle at my own little piece of naughtiness. I actually kept a copy of her original critique and when I saw the article you just spoke of, I sent a copy to her. I imagine she might think twice about demoralising up and coming young authors again."

"By the way, I am a big fan of your books as well. You have no idea how often I consult them to ensure I have incorporated the correct body movements for my characters, in an aim to animate them for my readers."

Sebastian's eyes open wide in surprise. "Well, I am certainly honoured. I can't wait to tell my wife I have met you as she is also an avid fan of your work. I have to apologise for changing the subject but as I explained on the phone, I'm here on official police business and I really do need to press on."

Of course, of course. Go ahead, Sebastian!"

"First of all, I'm a little curious why you became a parole officer?"

"Well you can thank Jacqueline for that. When she wrote that initial piece it hurt but, unlike those that would have thrown away their career at that point, I decided I needed to find a way of getting to know my killers and those who would have attachments to them. Once I became a parole officer it gave me that connection and as much as I hate to say it, I became a better writer for it."

Sebastian reflects on his past and how he had gone into the darker side of town to understand people from all walks of life when he was studying to become a psychologist.

"Would you mind telling me about an ex-client named James Hanigan?"

"I knew it! I knew this would be about him. What has he done? Has he hurt someone?"

Sebastian leans forward and rests one hand on top of the other which rests on his cane.

"No, it isn't like that at all. There was a recent homicide and the victim was a member of the gym, so we are doing routine interviews with friends, family and in this case, parole officer, who know any of the staff members there."

Samuel squints his eyes and his face fills with inquisitiveness. "The victim wasn't Michael Cohen, was it?"

Sebastian's eyes light up and he leans forward again to pick up his teacup, "As a matter of a fact it was; how did you know?"

This time Samuel's eyes light up. "Oh, my goodness! Oh, my goodness! Surely not? No, it can't be!" Samuel begins fanning his hand up and down in front of his face and Sebastian gives him time to collect himself.

Sebastian's forehead wrinkles, "What is it, what do you know?"

"When I first met Jamie, we would talk for hours about what had happened to get him into trouble, the people he had met inside the prison. At first I think I was more interested in him for the information that I could get for my books but when he confided in me that he was gay, I realised there was more to our relationship than I initially thought. The more we saw each the closer we become; eventually I realised something had to give, so I left my position as a parole officer and Jamie came and lived with me here. Anyway, one day he came home and he was absolutely beside himself, he told me that he had an altercation with one of the clients at the gym and his manager called him into his office and hauled him over the coals about it..."

Sebastian interrupts, "Yes, we know about that. Go on!"

"Well, his exact words were, 'if that had happened in prison, Michael Cohen would be laid out on a slab by now. He wouldn't be standing over the guys that live on the inside'." I told Jamie he needed to ignore people like that, which made him even angrier, and he told me I was too passive and that's why people like Michael get away with shit. One thing led to another and he picked up my beautiful Royal Dalton figurine and threw it into the wall, smashing it to pieces. That's when I ordered him out of my house and I told him I didn't want anything more to do with him, so he left. You don't think he did it, do you? Because I would blame myself for getting him the job there in the first place."

Sebastian looks at him through narrow eyes as he considers his next question. "It's still early in our investigations. But tell me, when you used to frequent the gym, can you remember anyone who had unusual characteristics?"

"There was one guy but he was only a delivery boy. He was always talking to Kate who owns the juice shop. I don't know why but the hairs on the back of my neck would stand up whenever he came near."

Sebastian pushes down on his cane and rises to his feet, "Well, I really have to be going so thank you very much for your help and for the wonderful cup of tea and cake."

"Wait! I have something for you" Sebastian stops in his tracks as Samuel heads into another room and returns with three books in his hands, "This one was my favourite books of yours; would you mind signing it?" Samuel hands him a pen.

"Thank you so much, Sebastian. Now, this is my new book that won't be on the shelves until next week. There's one for you and one for your lovely wife. Now would you like me to sign them?"

Sebastian's eyes light up like a little boy at Christmas, "Oh yes please! That would be wonderful!" After the books are signed and dated, Sebastian leaves the apartment smiling from ear to ear; he knows Cynthia will be over the moon with her special gift.

Out on the street, the wind is quite fresh and Sebastian inhales the aroma of freshly made doughnuts from the café next door. "I wonder how the boys and girls down the station would feel about a doughnut." He pays for two extra-large boxes filled to the brim. He places them on a nearby hydrant and holds them steady with one hand, as he frantically waves down cabs with his cane in the other. It's not long before one pulls up across the road but, to his dismay, a familiar gruff voice yells, "Well, FROSTY, do you want a cab or NOT!"

Sebastian looks through the blur of traffic hoping it's not who he thinks it is but it is and he is quick to reply, "JUST GO AWAY, WILL YOU!" He tries to hail other cabs but they just speed on by.

"You won't GET one, you KNOW" the driver persists from the other side of the road.

"AND WHY WOULD THAT BE SIR?" Sebastian replies with venom.

The cabby smiles and hangs one elbow out the window. "BECAUSE I RADIOED IN THAT YOU'RE MY FAIR; SO CAN YOU HURRY UP, I..."

Sebastian smirks in frustration, "I KNOW, I KNOW; YOU HAVEN'T GOT TIME TO MESS ABOUT WITH ME, BECAUSE YOU HAVE REGULAR CUSTOMERS TO TAKE CARE OF!"

"THAT'S RIGHT FROSTY And HERE'S a little tip for YOU... Look BOTH WAYS before you cross this VERY BUSY road," he breaks into laughter. Sebastian knows he hasn't got a choice, so he weaves in and out of traffic until he finally arrives on the other side. It's all a little much déjà vu for him. "Okay, you win. Now can we head back to the station?"

"Hang on a minute FROSTY; what's in the BOXES?"

"Doughnuts. Why?"

The cabby waves his head from side to side. "Sorry BUDDY, NO FOOD allowed in my cab."

Sebastian rolls his eyes. "You are jesting, surely?"

The cabby smiles, "Come ON, Frosty, do you think I would joke about something like THAT. Rules are RULES, you know? Well, MY rules anyway."

Sebastian is about to slam the door.

"Hang on a MOMENT, buddy, I do have one EXCEPTION to that rule."

Sebastian closes his eyes and takes a deep breath. "I hate to think what that would be but go ahead, surprise me!"

"When my REGULAR customers need to bring food in my cab I give them a twenty dollar surcharge. How does that sound to you?"

Sebastian's eyes nearly pop out of his head. "It sounds like bloody extortion, that's how it sounds to me!"

"Yes, I guess it is, now do you want the ride or not?"

Sebastian slides into the back seat. "What other choice do I have?"

"Good for you!" the cabby says as he turns to face the road ahead and starts the motor.

The trip is as quiet as the first one, apart from Sebastian's scribbling into a small notepad. On arrival Sebastian goes to open the door but the cabby quickly reaches around and grabs Sebastian's arm. "Not so fast, FROSTY! That will be ten bucks for the ride and twenty for carrying the food."

Sebastian grabs his cane and raps the driver over the knuckles with it. "I suggest you keep your hands to yourself and allow me to alight from your vehicle."

The cabby's eye's fire up and his grasp tightens. "You're not going anywhere, PAL, until you pay me my MONEY!"

Sebastian looks down at knuckles steadfastly holding his wrist and then glares with disgust. "I will give you one opportunity to remove your hand from my wrist before I take aggressive action."

"That's not going to happen, PAL, so give it your best SHOT!"

Sebastian grins evilly and reaches inside his jacket with his free hand. "Do you know what this is?"

The driver sneers "What, do I look STUPID? It's a PHONE! So what?"

"No sir, this is evidence. Evidence to prove what sort of rogue you really are." Sebastian pushes the play button and cabby eases his grip on his arm as he listens to a recording of the whole conversation. "Now, my good man, I would like you to observe where we are parked. It shouldn't take long, even with your limited intellect, to realise you are sitting outside a Police Station. A Police Station, where I just happen to work as a consultant for the Chief of Police." Sebastian gives the cabby a conquering smile. "As it has been a day of exchanging tips here is my tip for you, get your bloody hand off me and let me alight from this cab without having to pay a fee of any kind and I will reconsider my initial thoughts of taking this tape to my good friend and employer." The cab driver releases his grip and Sebastian grabs his belongings, steps out onto the curb and peers back in."Remember this... I am giving you the opportunity to correct the flaws in your attitude but I have taken your registration number just in case. Now my name is Sebastian Cork and I'm sure it will pop up from time to time in your travels."

"Oh, by the way, the doughnuts were bought for the hard working detectives within and I will let them know you have contributed to paying for them. I noticed on your registration your name is Mark Kramer; well, Mark, it's been not so pleasurable meeting you." Sebastian slams the taxi door and steps back from the curb as the driver burns rubber. He stands there waving his head from side to side; "I'm sure we will meet again," he says under his breath as he makes his way up the concrete steps.

Sebastian strolls through the building with a cheeky grin on his face, until he enters the room where most detectives type their reports and make calls. He places the boxes of goodies on a long table and stands on a wooden chair. "Excuse me, ladies and gentlemen!" Sebastian says as he waves his hands above his head. "I have brought you back some afternoon tea but before you partake, I need you to know I met this wonderful cab driver by the name of Mark Kramer who insisted that he contribute towards these delectable gems in gratitude for your hard work. He also asked me to inform you that, if you need a Cab anytime, you should ask for Mark, registration number four hundred and fifty-three, and he would be only too pleased to give you wonderful people a discount if you mention my name. Thank you for your patience. I hope you enjoy your doughnuts."

Gratitude fills the air and Sebastian heads towards the Dust Pit with a couple of doughnuts he has held back for Paul and himself.

++++

Paul is on Sebastian's side of the desk, working on notes after his meeting with Kate.

"Ahem, I brought you some afternoon tea."

Paul jumps up from Sebastian's seat and begins pushing his notes together. "Sorry, Seb! Hey they look great! Can I get you a coffee to have with them?"

Sebastian smiles. "I'd love one Paul, and while you're gone, it will give me an opportunity to type out some notes for you regarding Samuel James."

The phone peals. It's Cynthia.

"Hello, my dear! How has your day been so far?"

"Not too bad, Seb, but you probably only said that to be polite..."

Sebastian rears back like a bee has just stung him. "Hold on a minute! Before you go any further, my love, you are constantly reminding me that I'm not thoughtful enough and when I try to be, you act as though I really don't care."

Cynthia remains silent for a split second. "You are right, Seb. That was totally uncalled for."

"That's alright, my darling. Apology accepted. Now, what do you have for me?"

"It seems that you think I only ring when it has something to do with the case. Perhaps I rang just to say hello or had some important news of my own."

Sebastian can hear a wistful tone in Cynthia's voice and begins to worry, "Please, my love, what's wrong? You seem out of sorts."

I'm sorry, Seb. It's just been a day of ups and downs. I'll talk to you about it when you get home. In the meantime I researched Kate Kensington for you and here is what I have found out so far: Kate worked two jobs to pay her way through university and eventually became a qualified pharmacist. A few years ago she developed a new sports energy drink, 'KateEnergy' which she not only sells at her shop but distributes locally and nationally. Kate likes to attend seminars overseas especially ones related to sports drinks or foods. But the interesting thing is, her trips away coincide with each of the murders."

"Yes, that's very interesting! But let's put the case aside for now and talk about you..."

Before he can say anymore Cynthia cuts in, "Seriously. Seb, everything is okay and this isn't the time or place to discuss it. I will talk to you when you get home!"

Sebastian can hear the determination in her voice and decides not to push the issue any further.

"Alright, my love. I have about another hour left here then I will be on my way home."

Paul walks in with coffee just as Sebastian hangs up and sees the concerned look on his face. "Anything to do with the case, Seb?"

Sebastian, still looking perplexed at the phone, shakes his head. "Sorry Paul?"

Paul takes a seat, "The call; did it have anything to do with the case?"

Sebastian puts his phone back in his jacket, "Yes and no Paul; Now, tell me about your meeting with Kate."

Paul slumps back into his seat and begins to relate his morning meeting, as Sebastian listens and watches intently. "Well Seb, I did what you asked and observed her body movements, eased off when I felt things may be getting uncomfortable for her and listened to her words for any contradictions or hesitancies but I didn't find a lot of issues with how she addressed my questions.

"So are you saying there was nothing at all out of the ordinary?"

94

Paul inhales deeply, "Well I guess we all see things that don't fit in with other's thinking."

Sebastian peers through slit eyes, "Okay, so if we were to look at it from that perspective, what instances during the interview, made you feel things weren't quite, what they should be?"

Paul crosses his arms, tightens his lips and sinks his chin into his chest. "She did say something about elite sports people aren't all they're cracked up to be."

"What did you deduct from that comment? Remember you were acting as my eyes and ears and not your own."

"I felt it was said in a disrespectful manner rather than a passing comment."

Sebastian smiles with tight lips while maintaining a serious persona. "Excellent! Anything else?"

"Yes, there was one other thing; she spoke about travelling overseas but began tapping her fingers on the table and when I looked down at them, she seemed to become uncomfortable. In all honesty Seb, she doesn't take me as the serial killer type."

Sebastian braces his hands on the edge of the desk. "It's not for you to believe or disbelieve whether or not she is guilty and I can't make this any clearer than saying, a crime is a jigsaw puzzle and until all the pieces fit together in order to give us the bigger picture, we have nothing. Try not to put the puzzle together without all the pieces or it may lead you to having to cut the pieces to fit."

"You asked me earlier about my phone call and now I will tell you what Cynthia discovered; every time Kate has been away overseas, one of these horrific murders was committed."

Paul's eyes widen. "Then that proves she didn't do it?"

"No, Paul! It proves she has an alibi for each murder... but it is an amazing coincidence."

Anger shrouds Paul's face. "Seriously, Seb, I think you are brilliant at what you do but there are such things as coincidences, as you know and seriously, you really should back off Kate!"

Sebastian glares fire. "I suppose it's a coincidence that Kate is a chemist and the victim was given a drug. In a drink that most likely came from her shop? I suggest that sometime soon you get on your computer and type in 'countertransference'. That's all I have to say on this matter!" Sebastian begins collecting his papers together and putting them away in the drawer.

Paul unfolds his arms and screws up one side of his mouth, "So that's it, is it? End of the meeting because you have had enough?"

Sebastian rises to his feet and grabs his cane. "That, my friend, is the wisest deduction you have made thus far. I bid you good evening."

With that Sebastian rises to his feet, walks around his desk and out the door, leaving Paul wondering what the heck just happened.

++++

It has been an exceptionally long day and Sebastian's mind is racing like a hamster on a treadmill. Filled with thoughts about Paul's attitude and wondering what could be wrong with his precious wife; he can't help but sigh with relief when he passes through the gates that welcome him home. He sits in the car for a moment to clear his head of negative thoughts and then works his way along the tiled veranda where his beautiful brunette wife greets him with tears flowing down her cheeks; before he has a chance to console her, she throws her arms around him and sobs, "Oh Sebastian, I'm so glad you're home. I have so much to tell you!" He pulls her tight to him and kisses her on the forehead. "Come on, my love let's go in the kitchen and I will make you a chamomile tea and you can tell me all about it."

Sebastian gives his wife a solicitous glance while drawing a brown paper bag from his coat pocket. He haphazardly places his coat and cane on the hallstand and without further delay they make their way to the kitchen.

It's all very quiet except for the kettle as Cynthia collects herself and Sebastian waits impatiently for the water to boil. He pours them both a comforting brew. "There you are my love," he says as he places the steaming cup on the table in front of her. Sebastian takes a seat and gazes deep into her glazed eyes, "Now my love, what has caused this upset?" Cynthia begins to tear up again but takes a deep breath and exhales forcefully to settle herself down.

Her eyes narrow as she considers her answer and then all the concerns she has been carrying around internally come gushing out. "I know I should have told you, Seb, but I was frightened you may overreact. Anyway, here goes: four weeks ago, I felt a small lump in my breast so I went to my doctor and he decided to send me down to the hospital for a mammogram."

Sebastian begins to turn white and his eyes well with tears.

"Anyway, they found a small solid mass and Doctor Savage booked me for a day surgery to remove it; that's why I have been so sore around the chest area and not because I strained myself. Anyway, the results came back today..." Trying to be strong for his wife, Sebastian draws a handkerchief from his pocket and gently wipes his eyes, while she is staring down at her Tea.

"So tell me... what were the results, my love?"

She looks up into his eyes and sighs heavily, "Doctor Savage told me I had a benign tumour."

Sebastian can't hold back his tears anymore and they flow like raindrops down a window. "Thank God! Oh my love, don't ever hold things like this back from me again! No matter what the circumstances, I don't want you facing it alone. Come here!"

He stands and she walks into his arms sobbing uncontrollably. Once Cynthia collects herself she looks into Sebastian's eyes. "I knew, deep in my heart, I should have told you and I am so sorry. I promise you, I won't do that again. After losing my dear friend Margaret last year and seeing the devastation it caused Bill, I guess I panicked. Honestly, Seb, this whole thing has shaken me to the core."

Sebastian kisses her on the forehead again. "Of course it has and I am so glad you took the precautions you did by getting it seen to immediately." He rubs her shoulders gently and slowly and takes a deep breath.

They sit down and sip their tea while Sebastian listens empathically to Cynthia's ordeal in detail.

"What's that, Seb?"

She has caught him off guard and he stares blankly at her first and then turns his head around in the direction she is staring. "Oh that! I almost forgot, I have something for you."

Sebastian, obviously still quite shaken from her news walks nervously over to the bench and grabs the brown bag. "I went to Samuel James' apartment today."

"Oh yes, the parole officer."

Sebastian warmly smiles. "That's the one. Anyway, it turns out he's a bit of an author, so he gave me a couple of his new books that haven't been released yet, one for me and one for you. I read a bit of mine before I left the office."

"Is he any good?" she says, half interested.

"I will let you be the judge of that." He reaches into the bag and hands her the surprise.

Cynthia reads, 'To dearest Cynthia with warmest regards. Peter Karston.' She turns her astonished eyes to meet Sebastian's. "This can't be true, surely?"

"Trust me; I was just as surprised as you are." He sees the happiness in her face and contently smiles.

Cynthia rises from the table and throws her arms around him. "There are times when I could kill you, Seb, and there are times when you are worth more to me than the air that I breathe. I love you so much!" she says in a burst of spontaneous appreciation.

Sebastian holds her tight and feels his spirit meet with hers. That evening at dinner, they continue to discuss all the trials and tribulations Cynthia has faced over the past weeks and then retire to the study together to read; both content in the thought that the other is healthy and present in the same room. Later they go upstairs to their room and Sebastian falls asleep until he hears a muffled sob coming from Cynthia's side of the bed; so without speaking he moves closer to her and gently places his arm around her until they both fall asleep together.

Through the glare of morning sunshine and squinting eyes, Sebastian sees the silhouette of a slender beauty gazing down at him.

She bends slowly and kisses him, "Good morning, darling! I thought you might like a little sleep in today as you told me last night that there isn't anything urgent you need to attend to."

Sebastian stretches out his arms. "Mmm, what's that smell?"

Cynthia takes a tray from the dressing table. "Sit up, please. I wanted you to know how much I appreciated your support last night, so I thought you might like breakfast in bed and I brought up a plate of bacon and eggs, as well as some freshly squeezed orange juice."

Sebastian throws her a look of gratitude and accepts the feast. "How lovely! But seriously, Cynthia, you didn't have to go to all this trouble. I would have been just as happy to come down to the kitchen and share breakfast with you. But thank you, I do appreciate it."

Cynthia kisses him again. "Now I really have to have a shower and head off to meet Clarissa. I have an idea for a new fundraiser that I want to discuss with her and then we'll probably drive around most the day looking for a venue. So I may be home a bit after you. Since the scare I've just had, I'm sure we could raise a lot of money for cancer research. By the time, I get home it will be too late to cook, so I'll bring home some Chinese. How does that sound?"

Sebastian who now has a mouthful of bacon nods up and down, "wondorful thoort, mo lorve."

"Sebastian! Manners, please! You know better than to talk with your mouth full," she smiles at him and says, "Isn't it nice to have everything back to normal?" He smiles back with bulging cheeks, puts down his knife and raises his thumb.

After Cynthia has left, Sebastian has his shower, gets ready and heads downstairs for another coffee and a perusal of the morning paper but before he gets a chance to read more than the headline, he receives an incoming call: "Hi. Seb. It's Paul. I did a bit of research last night like you asked me to and I just want to apologise. It makes a lot of sense what you were saying and I really need to approach my work differently." Sebastian takes a slurp of coffee.

"What the hell was that, Seb? It sounded like a strong wind."

Sebastian had been told off once already for his bad manners. "No, that was just the radio, Paul. Thank you for your apology. This is why I feel you have great potential: because you are open to criticism without being emotionally unnerved."

"Thanks Seb, I appreciate that. Hang on a minute... where are you at the moment?"

"I am in the kitchen of my house, why?"

"You haven't got a radio in your kitchen; I know what that was - you were slurping coffee in my ear, weren't you!"

Sebastian exhales heavily. "Yes, Paul. If you really must know, I accidently slurped my coffee. Now, is there anything else I can help you with?"

"Yes, I just wanted to let you know that Chelsea's back in town for a few days so the chief gave me the okay for a rostered day off. I was going to let you know yesterday but you took off out of the office, so I didn't get a chance to. Is there anything you need from me?"

Sebastian smiles in a fatherly fashion. "No, actually that should work well. I'm going to the gym this morning and it's better if we weren't both there at the same time. Enjoy your day off and say hello to Chelsea from Cynthia and me; we can't wait to meet her."

"Thanks, Seb. That means a lot. Stay safe!" Sebastian throws down his coffee and grabs his coat and cane as he leaves.

By leaving later he has missed the peak hour traffic. Sebastian's in a much happier place than he was the day before, so he puts on the radio and begins to sing along. Lost in the overpowering joy he is feeling, he starts to bob and sway; that is, until he looks out his window and sees a police car driving alongside him.

The officer recognises him, flashes him a huge grin and a thumbs up. Sebastian turns crimson, rapidly turns his head and rigidly faces the windscreen. He flashes a peek to see if he's still got an audience; the policeman winks, gives him a loose salute and speeds off down the road.

"Why me?" Sebastian mutters out loud and then breaks heavily to avoid a car that has stalled in front of him.

He finally arrives at the gym in one piece and on entry finds it much warmer, so he throws his jacket across his arm and heads straight for Kate Kensington's shop but stops abruptly outside when he hears a familiar voice engaged in an argument. He takes up a position around the corner and out of sight. It's not long before Sally, Michael Cohen's fiancée, emerges and hurries to the exit, but Sebastian catches her by the arm. "Hello, Sally. Do you remember me?"

She jerks her arm away and eyes him up and down nervously. "Sure, you're the guy from the police station who was asking questions at the Cohen's house."

"Perhaps you can tell me how someone who doesn't know Kate Kensington very well happens to be having an argument with her?"

Sally closes her eyes and sighs. "Okay, I may have got off on the wrong foot by saying that Mike was getting too close to her and leaving off a few other details."

Sebastian looks at her sternly "Such as?"

"Just before Mike was murdered he told me he had bought a property from Kate and it was going to help him get out of financial difficulties. I thought, if I found the deed, I'd be able to help Mike's parents."

Sebastian can see she is telling the truth, "Where is this property, Sally? And did he buy it in his own name?"

"I honestly don't know. But I do know Mike wouldn't lie to me about something like this!"

"And what did Kate say about it?"

"She just played dumb like she knew nothing about it. I know she's lying, she has to be lying as I said, he wouldn't have told me if it wasn't true!"

Sebastian puts his hand on Sally's shoulder. "Please listen to me, Sally. When you do something like this it can jeopardise the whole case. I promise you if there is a deed I will find it but I need you to sit back until we have completed our investigation and, if anything else should come to mind, it's important that you let me know first. Can you promise me that?"

"I'll try."

Sebastian looks at her sternly. "No, Sally! I need you to promise, otherwise I will have to report this incident to my superiors; now, please, promise me!"

Sally's eyes drift from side to side, "Alright, I promise! Are you happy now?"

Sebastian nods gravely, "No Sally, I am not happy but it does give us a better chance of solving this heinous crime; so thank you."

Sally immediately scoops her head upward, "Whatever!" she sneers as she turns and walks out the door.

Sebastian enters the shop to find Kate on the phone. He watches her body expressions with great intent and listens closely. He's surprised how warm and fluid the conversation is. Normally Sebastian wouldn't think twice about it but her demeanour strikes him as a bit peculiar because Paul has told him that Kate's a loner. Sebastian also recalls she has no living relatives.

She glances over her shoulder for customers and her keen blue eyes meet Sebastian's. It's obvious he is observing her, so she finishes her call as quickly as possible and strolls up to the counter. "Sorry about that. Can I help you with something?"

Sebastian grins a little and replies probingly. "Not a problem at all... it's nice when family get in touch."

Her eyes once dead, now sharpen, making him feel uncomfortable. "I don't have any family to speak of. Now, can I get you something?"

The phone call has heightened his suspicion. "Ah, yes, one of those raspberry shakes thanks. It will help to kick start my day."

"Tell me something; is that patchouli oil I can smell?"

Kate looks sideways from the glass fridge while reaching for his drink. "Yes it is and, like everything else here, it's all natural."

Sebastian removes his wallet from his jacket. "I remember years ago when patchouli oil was all the rage. Do you get many people wanting it these days?"

"It's one of my more popular brands in essential oils. I wear it myself."

She's about to hand him his change when Sebastian holds up the palm of his hand. "In that case, I'd better get a bottle for my wife!"

"I guess women would be more interested in it thanmen," he says as she returns with the bottle.

"No, not at all. The guy that does my deliveries buys it all the time."Sebastian takes his drink and oil, thanks her and leaves. During his drive back he rings the Coroner to let him know he needs to meet with him urgently and on his arrival back at the station, he makes a B-line for his office.

++++

"Good morning, Cameron. How are you?"

Cameron looks up from the untidy mound of his desk, "Fine, thanks, Seb. How is that case of yours progressing?" He says with some disinterest as his eyes bounce all over his desk in search of something.

"It's moving along quite well, Cameron, but the reason I came down here to see you is this." Sebastian reaches into his pocket and pulls out the small bottle. He holds it up between his thumb and index finger and continues, "At Truscan Park we detected a familiar aroma?"

Cameron chuckles. "I remember! Sorry, Seb shouldn't laugh. But the look on your partner's face when you told him to smell it as well! Heh, anyway, enough of the frivolities! What do you need?"

Sebastian feeling some discomfort in not having the knowledge enquires, "Well, as you know, I'm new to all this… is there some way of comparing what's in this bottle to whatever substance is on the victim's tracksuit?"

Cameron holds out his hand. "Well, well, well, patchouli oil; this was all the rage years ago!"

"Yes I know. Is it possible to distinguish a connection?"

By bringing this little vial to us, we can compare it to the trace evidence and hopefully get the result you're looking for. So if you leave this with me, we will do some comparisons and see what we come up with."

Sebastian thanks Cameron and heads upstairs to Jim.

"Hi Seb," Emily greets him. "I was about to ring you. Jim wants to see you before he goes to the Commissioner."She rises to her feet, taps on Jim's door and enters. "Sebastian's here to see you Jim."

"Great send him in!"

Sebastian takes a seat while Jim busily shuffles through papers. "So, Seb?" Sebastian waits.

"I know you're covering good ground but what I need now is an accurate assessment of where we're at with this case so I can inform the Commissioner."

Sebastian crosses his arms and pushes his chin out. "Alright… but it is important that no conclusions are adopted prematurely - we all know what happened in the last case! I dare say the odds are in favour of that happening in this case as well. We all know our hierarchy are pushing for a rapid outcome."

Jim tucks his left arm under his right elbow and begins tapping his bottom lip. "I agree but I'm not so sure the Commissioner will. It may be better if you word your summary in a way that shows progress without implicating anyone person in particular; is that possible?"

Sebastian, calm and collected, replies, "I don't see why not."

Jim reaches into his desk drawer. "Just one more thing, Seb; I would like to record this. Do you mind?"

"Not at all, Jim. Would you like me to begin?" Jim presses record and nods.

"During our investigation, we found that a gym downtown may have a connection to all three murders. Now we have a link, it's a matter of sifting through evidence to pinpoint our culprit. Our next move is to do more interviews and one by one eliminate the innocent which will put pressure on the killer. Paul and I believe we are getting very close to closing this case and I feel confident that we will have this person in our grasp before another murder is committed."

Jim's eyes open wide. "That's a big call, Seb! How can you be so sure?"

Sebastian gives a cheeky grin, "I will let you know when the time is right, my friend."

Jim slumps back and shakes his head ruefully. "Honestly, Seb, if you were any other of my detectives, I would haul you over the coals. Now, I know full well the way you operate is something we, the force, need to look closely at, in the future but I will tell you one thing... if you screw this one up, I won't be able to hold back the stampede of political beef that will take you down to avoid being sent to the slaughter yards themselves."

Sebastian rises to his feet. "Honestly Jim, I only make statements that I am sure of and if I'm wrong, which I am not, I will make sure none of my mistakes are placed on your shoulders, as you have supported Paul and I throughout this case.

++++

When Sebastian arrives home, the house is eerily silent. Cynthia is nowhere to be seen and before he can even hang up his coat, his phone rings.

"Hi, Seb. It's Paul. I was wondering if you can take your car again tomorrow. I have to take Chelsea to the airport first thing in the morning and then go directly to the gym. Is that okay with you?"

Sebastian, still concerned as to Cynthia's whereabouts, replies impatiently. "Yes Paul, that's fine. I do apologise but I am in the middle of something and really have to go."

Sebastian hangs up, throws his coat and cane on the hallstand and moves toward her office with haste. "Cynthia, are you in there?" he opens the door to an empty room. "Bloody hell woman, where are you?" he says with serious concern as he heads back through the kitchen and toward the staircase. His breathing is getting heavier and fear washes over him. Halfway up the stairs he hears keys jingle outside the front door, so he races down to open it.

"Oh, my goodness! Sebastian, you scared the living daylights out of me!" She retorts, while still holding her keys toward the lock.

He glares back at his wife. "Scared you! Where the hell have you been?"

Cynthia angrily picks up several bags beside her feet. "Seriously, Seb! If I didn't have so much to do, I would take the time to throttle you!" She pushes past him on her march toward the kitchen.

He stands there momentarily contemplating what has just happened and then follows her to the kitchen.

As he walks through the door he sees Cynthia angrily unpacking boxes of Chinese takeaway. She quickly drops what she's doing, throws her hands on her hips and stares with venom straight into his eyes "Now... what's going on, Seb?"

Sebastian sighs, drops his head like a lost puppy and replies. "Well, my love, it seems I have been very remiss with my listening skills. I had fully forgotten that you were out with Clarissa today. When I got home and couldn't find you the worst possible scenarios began running through my head and I began to panic. I guess it was a bit of a reaction to your recent illness..."

Cynthia's emotions flow from anger to concern and can see he was sincerely frightened, so she holds out her arms to embrace him. "Okay. Just don't ever scare me like that again," she looks into his eyes and then gently kisses his lips.

Cynthia wakes, rolls over and shakes Sebastian's shoulder, "Time to get up, darling."

Sebastian turns to face her. "I don't think I'll go in 'til later, my love. I have a meeting with Paul this afternoon and I am well ahead of my bookwork, so I thought I might just spend the morning with you."

Cynthia gracefully throws back the sheets, goes to the wall, takes down a photo and lays it in the bed.

"Why did you put this in bed with me, Cynthia?"

She stands at the wardrobe sorting through her clothes and then glances back over her shoulder at him. "Because, my darling, my day is booked out again with Clarissa and if you want to spend the morning together, my photo is the only way to do that," she giggles and walks towards the bathroom.

Seconds later, she feels a soft blow between her shoulder blades and turns to see one of her pillows on the floor. She glances up at Sebastian, sitting upright with an enormous smile on his face. "Seriously Seb..? You can be a real child at times." She kicks the pillow back toward the bed and begins her journey again until another well-aimed missile hits her.

"Now you have done it..."

Sebastian begins to worry that he has pushed her too far.

"...if you want war you will have war! And I will shatter you!" Cynthia picks up both pillows from the floor and swings them into Sebastian with the momentum of a wrecking ball. As he tries to cover his head with his own pillow, she knocks it clean out of his hand and continues her barrage like a woman possessed. Sebastian holds his hands over his head and can't stop laughing and the more he laughs, the harder she hits until she is so weak from laughing and hitting, her arms and stomach ache. He grabs hold of her and rolls her over the top of him to her side of the bed.

They lie there giggling like two little children until she hears a crack. Cynthia pulls her photo from underneath her and the room becomes silent when she realises she has broken the glass on her photo.

"Who is shattered now, Cynthia?" Sebastian says dryly.

Cynthia dissolves into laughter and as she laughs she lets out a snort which makes both of them laugh even louder and longer. She begins picking up the shards of glass from the bed and a tear comes to her eye as she looks lovingly at her husband. "Thank you, Seb! I've been so stressed over the past few weeks that I had forgotten how to laugh. You always come through for me when I need you most!"

"Ditto, my love. Ditto!" Cynthia snatches her clothes up off the floor and hurries into the shower. By the time she returns, Sebastian is fast asleep. She kisses him gently on the cheek and leaves for her big day with Clarissa.

++++

While Sebastian sleeps, Paul has already dropped Chelsea off at the airport to catch her very early flight and is now motoring his way to the gym. On arrival he quickly works his way to the change rooms with the intent to be at the station by nine.

Just as he finishes changing, another fellow enters. "Hi, how are you? I'm Jamie. I saw you working out the other day and it looks like you've been around a gym before." He extends his arm.

Paul shakes his hand and smiles, "Hi, Jamie. Good to meet you, I'm Paul. I'm from out of town; this is a bit of a fill in until I get back to my own gym."

Jamie nods. "Well, I'm one of the personal trainers here so if there's anything I can help you with, I'm your man. Though I can tell by your form you probably won't need much advice from me."

"Well, none of us are perfect. We should never pass up the opportunity to learn. I certainly don't envy the job you do, though. I've met some really arrogant jocks; I bet you've come across a few?"

Jamie's face relaxes. "Definitely! As much as we don't like to speak ill of the dead, I came across a guy who fits that category perfectly."

Paul turns his lip up at one side. "I hear you loud and clear, he was probably one of those pretenders too... you know, makes out they're champions but in reality, can't make the grade."

Jamie pulls a key from his pocket, opens his locker and rests his hand on the top of the door. "On the contrary, Paul, he was a champion tri athlete. But a shocking bigot when it came to homosexuality!" He reaches in his locker for his workout gear. "Sorry... I've probably said too much," he says apprehensively.

Paul holds his right palm up. "No, not at all. We're all born different. Short, tall, white, black, gay or grey, we all swim in the same pond so it's not that important to me if you're gay. So long as you're okay with me being hetero, we'll get along fine."

Jamie smiles. "Then I guess we're going to get along fine."

Paul sees an opening, "So what did this fellow do?"

"As usual, I was moving around the gym checking if everyone was being seen to, when I noticed this guy misusing the equipment in the way he was lifting. I was concerned he might hurt himself, so I pointed out the mistake he was making. Anyway, he looked me straight in the eye and said, "What would a faggot like you know?" I could see by the look in his eye he wasn't going to listen to me, so I started walking away and the next minute, BANG! I'm hit in the back of the head with a full water bottle."

Paul keeps the momentum going, "What a sick bastard! I don't know if I could hold back; I think I would retaliate."

Jamie sighs, "I did, worse luck! I grabbed him by the throat and as much as I hated the guy, because of the grief he caused me, I feel bad for doing it now he's gone."

Paul heeds Sebastian's words and backs off in order not to raise suspicions. "You know, you really shouldn't be so down on yourself; whatever happened was meant to be. But, hey, thanks for taking time out to introduce yourself."

Jamie smiles as Paul taps him with the open hand on the way out, "I will catch up with you around the gym and yell out if you need anything Paul."

Paul doesn't turn but holds his hand up in acknowledgement "Will do!"

Paul has been working out for a couple of hours and he is just about to leave when he spots Joe Devonport heading toward the exit. He's only a small slim fellow, moving at good pace, and Paul needs to hasten to catch him. "Hi, Joe. Can I have a word?" he says as he latches hold of Joe's gym bag.

Joe comes to an abrupt halt and wrenches his bag out of Paul's hand, "Who the fuck are you?" he says in a high-pitched voice, glaring daggers. Paul works hard to keep a straight face at Joe's tenor voice and the oversized beanie he's wearing doesn't help either. His button nose is covered in rather large freckles and Paul thinks he'd make a perfect pantomime character.

"I'm a friend of Kate's and because I'm new, she suggested you might introduce me to some of the people that work out here."

Joe, who seems to be in a hurry to get somewhere, snaps back at Paul, "What sort of a friend?" pulling at the neck of his shirt to straighten it.

"No, buddy, you've got it all wrong. Kate's been helping me to meet people around here, that's all. As lovely as she is, she's not my type and I mean that in the nicest possible way."

Joe's demeanour changes and he lets his bag slide onto the floor. "Sorry about that. I was in a bit of a hurry, that's all. Look, if you meet me here at six tomorrow, I'll walk you around, okay?" Joe shakes Paul's hand and heaves the heavy gym bag back over his shoulder. "Okay?"

Paul's eyelids lower and a questioning expression falls slowly over his face. "That would be good, Joe. I'll see you then." Paul has had enough for the morning, so he showers, changes and heads back to the station.

++++

Sebastian arrives at the station an hour after Paul and says his routine good morning to the policeman at reception who gives a half smile as he grabs his phone to make a call. Sebastian drops his cane with a crack and everyone looks up. He picks it up and continues on his way to the Dust Pit, only to find Paul in high spirits after typing up his report."Hi, Seb, here's a coffee for you; how has your morning been?" he says cheerfully.

"Good, good and thank you for my coffee. Oh, by the way, I suggest you sit up straight as Jim is on his way here, "he replies in a serious manner.

Paul quickly looks up from checking over his paperwork, "What? Here in the Dust Pit?"

Jim knocks on the door opens it and half enters, "I'm glad you're both here." Paul looks in disbelief firstly behind him at Jim and then back at Sebastian. He tilts his head and opens his hands covertly while looking at Sebastian curiously."

Sebastian, who is taking a seat, gives him a wink and relaxes back in his chair, arms crossed. "How long have we got, Jim?"

Jim's skin creases between his eyebrows. "What do you mean?"

Sebastian lifts his eyes slowly to the ceiling and then back down again. "I mean, the meeting with the Commissioner didn't go as well as you hoped and he has set a timeframe to wind up this investigation."

"How the …"

"Let's look at the facts, Jim. I gave you an update yesterday so you're not here on a fact-finding mission. Now, normally, if you needed us, for a matter, you'd send Emily to fetch us. It has to be about the case because you want to talk to both of us. So where does that leave us?"

"I picked up the morning paper on my way in and Michael Cohen's face was plastered all over it. I imagine the Commissioner was informed before it was released… and you had a meeting with the Commissioner, after which you informed reception to ring you as soon as I arrived. So here you are - about to inform us that the Commissioner has locked in a timeframe for you to bring more investigators onto the case." Sebastian expounds.

Jim leans heavily up against the door frame and smiles. "How could you be sure the guy on reception was contacting my office?"

Sebastian smiles confidently and then a veil of seriousness falls over his face. "Well, normally, he greets me with a smile and a casual salute but this morning he had a nervous half smile and quickly grabbed the phone. I gave him a questioning stare and, once I saw his head bow with guilt, it was good odds that he was phoning about me. So I deliberately dropped my cane and as I bent to retrieve it, I saw that he was ringing Emily's extension and when she didn't come to meet me before I reached the Dust Pit… well, anyway, you're here now. How long do we have?"

Jim tightens his lips. "No more than a week, I'm sorry."

Sebastian smiles in a fatherly fashion, "That is not a problem, Jim. Paul and I will have this investigation wrapped up in a matter of days."

Paul's face contorts as though he has tasted something bitter on hearing Sebastian's statement and before long it turns to a negative frown. Jim nods his head gently. "You know something… I believe you guys will." Jim turns to walk out and then turns around again. "Oh, by the way, we have just had an increase in the budget for construction and I've put in for an extension to the Dust Pit. So keep your fingers crossed." Jim turns again and strolls out.

Paul slumps back in his chair. "Are you kidding me, Seb?"

Sebastian stares at him inquisitively. "No. What would I be kidding about?"

Paul looks through sharp peering eyes, "How the hell are we going to tie this up in a few days?"

Sebastian smirks. "I never said a few days; I said a matter of days. I'm not sure whether you know this or not but there are three hundred and sixty-five days in a year and that's all that matters."

Paul waves his head as it bows. "This isn't a joke, Seb. The pressure is on."

Sebastian's smile fades from his face. "No, Paul. The pressure is on someone who is unwell or can't cope with everyday life. We are the fortunate ones! We have our health and prosperity and it's about time you started to believe in achievability. We just have a few loose ends to tie up and we will close this case in a matter of days. Now, can we talk about your morning at the gym, please?"

Paul relaxes again and talks at length about the conversations he had, especially about Jamie Hanigan and Joe Devonport. Later that day before they leave Sebastian tells Paul he will visit Joe's old neighbourhood in the morning and as Cynthia is busy with Clarissa, he makes numerous calls until he eventually tracks down Joe's old address. Paul tells Sebastian he will spend another day at the gym.

++++

Sebastian makes a couple of stops on his way home and on arrival puts his packages down, removes his coat and heads for the kitchen where he can hear the giggling of female voices. "Hello, what are you two up to?" Cynthia and Clarissa are working on invitations at the kitchen table and they both look up at him then smile at each other while Sebastian stands there with a questioning look on his face. "Anyway, I brought you something, my love." He draws a bunch of beautiful red roses from behind his back.

Clarissa's eyes light up and Cynthia gets to her feet and gives him a welcoming kiss, "Awe! Thank you, Seb! I'll find an empty vase for these; what else do you have there?"

"Well, unlike yesterday, I remembered you and Clarissa were meeting today and I was hoping you would both end up back here like you sometimes do," he smiles at Clarissa and then continues.

"Now, I know your wonderful husband is away at the moment, Clarissa, so I dropped into this fantastic little Japanese restaurant on the way home and bought enough for the three of us; would you do the honour of joining us?"

Cynthia smiles at him lovingly and Clarissa replies with a big cheeky grin, "Thank you so much, Seb, but I will have to decline unless I can put a condition on it."

"Definitely my dear. What is it you require?"

She glances over to Cynthia. "Well... I thought we might have a good old fashioned pillow fight after we have eaten." Both women break into fits of laughter and Sebastian, although trying hard to maintain a little dignity, eventually weakens and creates a trumpeting noise with his lips. The rest of the evening is spent in joyous laughter and frivolities.

As Sebastian drives toward the inner city he notes the change in scenery. Scents of industry from factories and warehouses litter the area. The smell mixes with an aroma of fresh food and coffee. It then dissipates, only to reappear as steel dust, rust and diesel from the railway line that seems to have magically appeared which is now running parallel to the road. The tracks eventually snake off in another direction; which leaves Sebastian feeling isolated as they had made him feel like they were along for the ride. The streets in Joe's old neighbourhood are lined with tarred pavements and bluestone edging and many of the townhouses of red brick with cream are crammed together like a line of sentinels guarding secrets from bygone days.

Sebastian pulls over to the curb, grabs his cane from the car and strolls onto the tiled veranda. He knocks on the door where Joe had lived with his family and feels a cold rush go up his spine, making the hairs on the back of his neck tingle.

A young blonde woman, wearing casual clothes and no makeup, answers the door. "Yes, can I help you?" she says apprehensively.

Sebastian shows her his identification. "I sincerely hope so. I'm wondering if I may have a word with you. I promise I won't keep you long. I'm helping the police with an investigation and I thought you might be able to tell me a little about the people who lived here before you?"

She backs away slightly and her eyebrows knit. "I'm not in any danger, am I?"

"No, no, not at all. This is just a routine investigation, nothing to worry about," he replies in his deep, dulcet voice.

So with begrudging approval, she continues. "I'd rather do this interview with my husband present but as there's not a lot I can tell you, it really won't matter all that much. All I can say is that, when we first moved in, the neighbours kept telling us how grateful they were that we were here and that the Devonport's had moved out."

"Did they say why?"

She sighs a little with annoyance. "Now this isn't coming from me so I don't want any repercussions, I'm only telling you what the neighbours told me.

From what they said the police or child safety were called two to three times a week to take care of the domestic issues; apparently he would bash her and she would take it out on the boy. That's all I know but from what I'm told, Mrs Green four doors down knows more. Just don't tell her I told you!"

He assures her he won't, thanks her and heads off down the street.

Sebastian leaves the car where it is as he feels the need for exercise – after all, it's only four doors down – and he shortly arrives at a quaint red and blue brick Victorian. Just as he opens the white wire gate, the lace curtains twitch and an old woman peers out from the side of them. He raises his cane in a friendly manner and the curtains vigorously swing closed.

Unperturbed Sebastian turns and shuts the creaking gate and continues his way up the path. He finds himself overwhelmed by the fragrance of the beautiful cottage garden and its splendid design of ruby velvet roses, lilac lavenders and the sweet perfumed jasmine that runs along the fence line. He inhales for one last time then follows the brick path up to the heritage green door. He turns the winged metal doorbell and hears dainty footsteps within. The door half opens and a frail figure of a woman pops her head around like a child playing hide and seek behind a tree.

She pulls her chin tight against her neck, cautiously looks up and her voice quavers with age. "Who are you and what can I do for you?" Sebastian goes to hand her official papers but before he can extend his arm fully, "I don't want whatever you are about to hand me. Now, I asked you a question, Sir. Who are you and what do you want?"

Sebastian surprised by her change from frail to assertive, places the papers back into his jacket, "I do apologise Mrs Green, my name is Sebastian Cork..."

Before he can speak another word the door flings wide open. "I knew it! You're a bit older now but I knew it! Well, don't stand there. Come in, come in!"

Now Sebastian's the curious one. He follows the frail hunched figure down the narrow, musty, hallway to a kitchen where she begins filling her kettle. She tells him to take a seat as she hobbles into another room. "Here it is!" a muffled voice is heard from the other room and the shuffling footsteps grow as she works her way back to the kitchen. Mrs Green holds up a large book with Sebastian's photo on it.

"This is your first book and the only one with your picture on the cover; I never forget a face and yes, you were a lot younger then, but I knew it was you the moment you came through that gate. Oh, how I wish Elsie was still alive; she'd be screaming and carrying on like a banshee at Halloween. We both studied psychology at the same university, and after our graduation remained friends 'til poor Elsie passed a couple of years back. "The kettle begins to whistle and the old woman turns off the gas. "You know something? We could see you were special after reading your first book and as soon as you brought out a new edition, Elsie and I would sit and discuss the essence of it. Your career bonded our friendship and I can't thank you enough. Now, what would you like, tea or coffee?"

Sebastian's been so tied up with his police work of late, he rarely has time to reflect on his past career. If most others were presented with the highest award in the field of psychology, it might change the way they see themselves but not Sebastian. It seems to have no real bearing on the 'here and now' and even the books he's presently writing are focused on the criminal mind, an area he has never fully delved into before. Her flattering spiel has pleased him enormously and he didn't blink an eye as he replies, "Coffee would be great. Thanks, Mrs Green. My goodness me, I am surprised anyone would remember that book. Your kind words are overwhelming, thank you!"

"Call me Olive, it's short for Olivia. As far as you being surprised, perhaps a little, but overwhelmed, definitely not."

He folds his arms and looks into her eyes. "What do you mean?"

This time her lips push her cheeks upward as her smile broadens further. "Look at you with your arms crossed and a frown on your forehead! There's really no need to get defensive! Now if you had fidgeted with your collar, or even raised your eyebrows a bit, I may have agreed that you were overwhelmed but those steely eyes gave you away."

Sebastian unfolds his arms and breaks into laughter. "Very good, Olive! You have not only been reading my books, you've also been using my theories to your own advantage. Well done, you!"

She confidently takes a seat at the table with him, opens a tin that contains homemade fruit cake and pushes it toward him. "So what brings you here, Mr Cork; are the neighbours trying to get me put away?"

He takes a piece of cake. "Sebastian. You can call me Sebastian. No, it's nothing like that. I'm actually a consultant for the police these days, and I just wanted to ask you if you remember a fellow by the name of Joe Devonport? His family lived four doors down from here."

She begins pouring him a coffee and a worried frown eclipses her exceptionally smooth forehead. "Is he behind bars?"

Sebastian squints at the question. "No. This is just an enquiry, that's all."

She goes to the refrigerator without saying a word, then returns with a small ceramic jug of milk. Before she withdraws a chair to sit opposite him, she rests both her hands on the back of it and takes a deep breath. "That's a long time ago, Sebastian, and if you don't mind, I'd rather change the subject."

Sebastian can see she's frightened; all the same, he doesn't waste his words. "I'm happy to do that for a short time, Olive. But I'm on the clock and will need to leave shortly. I hope you understand."

She shrinks back into her chair. "Yes, of course. But can you tell me, what made you leave your brilliant career so soon after achieving the highest accolade in the field of psychology? You were at the pinnacle of your career!"

Sebastian feels he owes her an explanation, especially since she has followed his career for so long. "Honestly Olive, I was turning sixty. Yes, I was at the apex of my career, and perhaps that's the reason I was feeling the lack of challenge in my life. All I knew at the time was: I needed a break. The thrill I had for my career was dwindling and that couldn't be good for my clientele or my students. My wife, in all her wisdom, believed I had more to offer than just retirement and providence provided the solution."

A client's brother was murdered and the police were understaffed. Although I was saddened for my client's loss, I felt thrilled and excited at the new challenges the case would bring. And I have never since regretted the path I took as it has breathed renewed energy into this old man."

Olive tilts her head toward her shoulder and waves it gently from side to side, "Yes I still have the paper clippings from when you solved the murder. Look Sebastian, I know I haven't been much help but there are some things even Psychologists don't get over." She gets up from the table, goes back to the refrigerator and grabs a pen and notebook from the top of it, then returns and begins jotting down some notes, "This is the phone number and address of Joe's old headmaster. He's retired now but I'm sure he'll be able to help you more than I can." She rips the page from the notebook and hands it to Sebastian.

"I understand Olive, and thank you."

She places both her hands over his, and, in an emotional voice replies, "No, thank you! Not just from me but from Elsie as well, God rest her soul." Olive sees him out to the gate where they say their goodbyes and Sebastian plods steadily onwards in the direction of his car.

No sooner does he open the Bentley's door, throw his cane in the back and sit in the driver's seat then he receives a call from Cameron Buckley. "Hi, Seb. I have just received the results back on your patchouli oil and it is an exact match. As usual you have hit the nail on the head, my friend."

A large smile eclipses Sebastian's face. "Thank you so much, Cameron. I appreciate the good work you and your staff do; it makes this job so much easier."

"No problems, Seb. Have a great day." Sebastian hangs up the phone and then reads the name and address written on the paper Olive has given him. It reads 'Henry Collins- 58 Sampson way Ph.79582123' and even though Cynthia has been constantly on his back to use a GPS, there are some things he has trouble changing; so he pulls his book of maps from the glove compartment and sees the address is only a block from where he is now.

Sebastian rings Henry to let him know he's coming and then begins his short journey through the narrow streets and arrives near his house within a matter of minutes. It's quite a busy little district with very few places to park and Sebastian is angry with himself for not walking from where he was originally. He eventually finds a spot further up the street, parks the car, grabs his cane and strolls along the well-worn pavement to the old principal's home.

As he passes through yet another creaking gate and up the glazed red brick paved path toward the house, a tall solidly built balding man wearing circular wire glasses opens the front door and greets him at the entrance. He extends his arm to shake Sebastian's hand. "Hi, I'm Henry and you must be Sebastian. Come in, come in." Henry leads him halfway up the hallway and then veers off into a quaint little lounge room with paintings hung on every wall. "Take a seat, Sebastian. My wife's out shopping at the moment and we don't have much in the way of biscuits or cake until she gets back but can I offer you a tea or coffee?"

Sebastian eases back into the comfort of the antique lounge chair and rubs his hands up and down the smooth French oak at the front of the arms. "No, I'm fine thanks, Henry; I just had one but thanks anyway."

Henry collapses back into the chair opposite and rests his hands across his stomach by interlocking his fingers. "I received a call from Olive straight after I got off the phone with you. She tells me I'm in the presence of one of the greatest psychologists there ever was; is this true?" he says as his wrinkled face takes on an inquisitive surveillance.

Sebastian pushes his chin up and looks at the ceiling, then begins rubbing the hair on the back of his head with the tips of his fingers. Sometimes he wishes his past achievements could remain in the past but it seems fame always comes with a price.

Henry can see his question has put Sebastian out of sorts and is quick to rectify his mistake. "Sorry, Sebastian. I didn't mean to make you feel uncomfortable; what can I help you with?"

Sebastian slowly drops his head back down and places his index finger across the top of his upper lip and his thumb beneath his chin. "No, please, don't apologise and no, I don't believe I'm the most famous. Don't get me wrong - I am good at what I do but sometimes life throws some people more opportunities than it does others. As for what it is you can do for me, I'm wondering if you recall a young boy who attended your school, his name is..."

Before Sebastian can finish his sentence Henry completes it for him. "Joe Devonport. Yes, I remember him well. Olive also told me why you were coming here and gave me permission to inform you why she had been so apprehensive about communicating her experiences with Mr Devonport. Back then there used to be a warehouse down the bottom of Olive's street. I'm pretty sure there's a car yard there now. Anyway, Olive used to go there to feed the stray cats that would amass in and around it for shelter. One particular evening she went down there and found Joe torturing one of the strays; in fact it was so badly mutilated she had to take it to the vet to be put down. Olive knew the school blazer he was wearing and came to my office the following day to report what she'd seen. I was appalled at what she told me and I immediately called Joe to my office while Olive was still there. I thought if he saw her in the flesh he would confess. I still regret my decision to have her present as it was a huge mistake."

Sebastian becomes curious. "What makes you say that, my friend?"

Henry continues, "I don't know if she told you but Olive was a fairly prominent psychologist around here and she had done some counselling work for some of the students previously. That's how I knew she wasn't exaggerating about what she'd seen but the moment Joe strode into my office as cocky as all get out, he began denying her whole story. In fact, he then threatened her by saying that if she kept saying things about him there would be consequences. I ended up giving him detention just for his attitude but there was nothing else I could do, it was her word against his. Anyway, Olive had a cat of her own that she'd let out at four every afternoon and it would always come back at five for a feed but the day she visited the school the cat went out and didn't return that evening. She found it the next morning wired to her gate and mutilated so badly it had choked on its own blood; suffice to say Olive hasn't had a cat since."

Sebastian sits forward in the chair. "That explains Olive not wanting to discuss Joe. Tell me, were there any other incidents at the school involving Joe that you know about?"

Henry curves the corner of his lips on one side and nods gently in the affirmative. "When Joe first came to the school he seemed to have a needy air about him but overtime he began to show an inner evil strength. Some things were brought to my attention by my staff and I dealt with them as I would any other issues regarding pupils but after the episode with Olive, I kept a very close eye on him. There were further incidents that we believed Joe was possibly involved in where a couple of boys had been cut by a very sharp object and even the police were called in to investigate but we believe the boys were so frightened of what Joe might do, they said they had been playing with broken glass and cut themselves. I was convinced there was more behind it than what they were saying, so I put him on watch even during recess but he was smart enough not to try his antics inside the school grounds again."

Sebastian pinches his bottom lip and then sways his head in disapproval. "What about his parents, Henry? I was told that violent domestic quarrels were a regular event in their house and were often followed up with the boy getting a beating?"

"What you heard is more than likely correct Sebastian; advocates from the child safety department would regularly come to the school to check up on him as they were getting nowhere with the parents. Each time someone was sent to the house to investigate the matter, they were told the boy was clumsy and always falling over, so they approached Joe as well and he would back up his parents' claims."

Without warning Sebastian cuffs his hands over his cane which is resting between his legs and pushes himself up to his feet, "Well I can't thank you enough, Henry. Your information will help me build a fairly good profile but I really must be on my way now."

Henry sits to attention and then rises to his feet and moves to shake Sebastian's hand. "Tell me something, Sebastian, what's this all about?"

Sebastian grasps Henry's hand and holds it steadfast. "Henry, I'd love to tell you but as you know some things need to remain confidential."

Henry grabs the back of Sebastian's right hand with his left and smiles cheekily. "Of course... but no harm in trying."

Sebastian smiles back. "None at all Henry; none at all. Oh, by the way, Henry...do you know if a flea has any significant meaning for Joe?"

Henry releases Sebastian's hand and affirms Sebastian's question by nodding his head. "Unusual question but the answer is yes. It was a nickname the older boys gave him because of his height. They never used it in a way to belittle him in front of others – well not that we saw anyway – and it never seemed to bother him, so we didn't see it as bullying."

Sebastian deep in thought remains emotionless and without blinking an eyelid he begins his walk to the front door. Once there he turns and shakes the retired Head Master's hand again. "Thanks again, Henry. I appreciate your hospitality and information. "Henry smiles and waits on the porch until Sebastian is through the gate before he goes back in.

Sebastian strolls back toward his car while remaining deep in thought, so deep in thought in fact, he walks straight past it and doesn't realise 'til a passing ambulance with its sirens blaring jump starts him back into the real world. He finally returns to his car, throws his cane in the back and takes out his phone from inside his jacket. It has been a long day so he decides to ring Paul and tell him he will be going straight home, rather than calling into the station.

That evening Sebastian is uneasy as he sits eating dinner with Cynthia. His thoughts are fully consumed with what he has learned about Joe and contemplating if it is possible for someone like Kate to be in two places at the same time. He filters and sorts through all types of scenarios and vague possibilities that rapidly run through his mind like sand in an hourglass and will only shut down his thinking process once the improbable has been totally eliminated and the most plausible of all results is achieved. Whenever he's in this deep mindset, Sebastian tends to hit a switch within that shuts him off from all that is happening around him.

Cynthia, who knows him better than anyone, stops chewing, puts down her knife and fork and slumps back in her chair. "Okay, Seb, what's going on in there?" she says with a mixture of annoyance and concern.

Sebastian, who is separating peas with his knife and then scrambling them again with his fork, is drawn from his thoughts by her probing question. "Sorry, my love. I was just thinking about the case and there are quite a few things that aren't making any sense whatsoever."

She smiles within, knowing it wasn't so long ago that he was contemplating retirement and how it would have been a great loss if he hadn't found this newborn enthusiasm working with the police department. "Is there anything I can help with?" she asks sincerely, as she leans forward to pick up her utensils again.

"It would help me immensely if you could make a few phone calls for me tomorrow."

She gives him a small grin and says, "That won't be a problem, Seb. Just write out the details after we finish our dinner; all I need to know is who you want me to ring and what you want to know and I will get onto it first thing tomorrow."

After dinner Sebastian has to be reminded by Cynthia about the list of information he requires, so he goes to his office, types up his requests and then returns to spend the rest of the evening discussing the case with his wife in the study.

The following morning during his drive to the station, Sebastian receives a call from Paul. "Hi, Seb. I'm on my way to the gym now and I might spend a full day there, so I will ring you when I finish and we can debrief over the phone if that's alright with you?"

"That will be fine Paul; I will talk to you later."

Sebastian continues his journey without interruption to the station and on arrival he heads straight to the Dust Pit, where he spends several hours reading through all the notes from the previous day and then typing out an updated file for Jim.

Once complete he goes to Jim's office and Emily tells him that he has just missed Jim as he has gone out to lunch. Sebastian leaves his report with her and works his way back to the Dust Pit. Just as he takes a seat at his desk his phone rings.

"Hi, Darling. Wow, this was a hard one! But I think the information I have for you is just what you are looking for."

"Wonderful! Go ahead, my love."


Cynthia continues with enthusiasm. "Well, apparently during Kate's travels overseas, she has been accompanied by a young boy who has cerebral palsy; his name is Dylan McConkey."

Sebastian scratches his head. "That is interesting, my dear, and such an unusual surname at that."

Cynthia is quick to reply. "Yes that's what I thought, so it wasn't hard for me to find out where he lives with his mother whose name is Michelle. As soon as we get off the phone I will text you the details of their address."

Sebastian thanks his wife, hangs up and waits for his personal message to come through.

Once he has the address, he works his way out of the building, jumps in his car and drives to Michelle McConkey's apartment but finds there is no one at home.

Sebastian makes some quick calls and then gets on the phone to Cynthia again. "Hello, my darling. I'm sorry to bother you but I need you to look up someone else rather urgently please; in fact it could be a matter of life and death."

Cynthia is temporarily quiet and then replies, "You aren't in danger, are you Seb?"

"No my love but someone – I'm not sure who but someone – is if I can't get this done quickly!"

"I'll get onto it immediately, Seb, and send you through another text as soon as I can get the answers."

No sooner does Sebastian get off the phone to Cynthia then he is on the phone to Jim and asks him for a couple of favours. Sebastian's mind is ticking over like a well-oiled machine, as everything begins happening in quick succession and immediately after getting off the phone to Jim, he receives his message from Cynthia and then jumps in his car again and speeds off.

++++

Meanwhile, at the gym, it has been another day of Paul working his way around the complex while talking to people and trying to get as much information as possible. He spies Joe Devonport near the weights and feels this might be a good time to delve a little deeper. "Hi, Joe. How are things? I thought you were going to help me meet people today, what happened?"

Joe's mouth contorts slightly and his pupils glare upwards from below a crinkled frown. "Sorry, I got busy with deliveries. Work has to come first you know."

Paul gives a gentle nod of his head and smiles with closed lips. "Fully understand, pal; we all have our priorities." Paul moves to the exercise bikes which are right next to where Joe is shining up some of the gym equipment."Hey, Joe? Someone over there was telling me that another guy from the gym was murdered the other week; did you know him?"

Joe looks at Paul out of the corner of his eye and continues cleaning. "Yes, I knew him. Why?"

Paul starts peddling a bicycle he has just mounted and continues to dangle the bait out to see if Joe will bite. "Just curious, that's all. It's not a common occurrence that someone from the same Gym you attend is murdered; now is it?"

Joe, still polishing, seems reluctant to respond. "Guess not."

Paul continues obstinately, "What was he like?"

Joe swings his head around and glares at Paul with piercing eyes but before he can answer, Kate comes over to join in on their chat. "Hi, boys. I brought you over a free drink each because I'm closing the shop early today and taking the next couple of days off."

"Going anywhere in particular, Kate?" Paul asks with a smile.

She glances over at him while handing the drinks to Joe. "Yes. As a matter of a fact I am, Paul, I have an interstate seminar to attend and I have to be at the airport in a couple of hours, so I better get a move on."

Joe smiles, "Safe trip, my friend."

Paul follows suit. "Yes, safe trip, Kate. I'll see you when you get back."

Kate looks back over her shoulder as she begins to head off. "Thanks, boys. Enjoy your drinks and I will see you in the not so distant future."

Paul begins pedalling again and Joe moves a machine further over and continues his cleaning. After awhile Paul has worked up a sweat and decides to hit the showers. "Hey, Joe. Do you have that drink that Kate left me? I've had enough and it's getting late."

Joe scurries over with Paul's drink. "There you are," he says as he extends his hand out with the KateEnergy in it.

"Thanks, I needed this," Paul replies as he takes a large swig of the elixir and then continues, "You never told me what this guy that got murdered was like."

Joe glares at Paul as he did earlier. "Not now! I'll have more time to talk about it tomorrow; as you can see I have to finish cleaning this machine and then I'm heading home myself."

Paul gets off the bike and peers over his shoulder at Joe. "Alright, Joe, I will see you tomorrow."

Paul realises that time has got away from him, so he throws down a good wash of the drink that Kate left and then quickly heads back to the change rooms to ring Sebastian and let him know he will catch up with him in the morning. Just as he is about to call he realises he had forgotten to charge his phone the night before and his mobile is dead. "Shit! Oh well, he would have left by now anyway," he mumbles to himself but unknown to Paul, Sebastian is still at the station and is trying desperately to contact him. Paul showers before leaving the gym and as he's getting dressed he loses balance and almost falls. "Wow, really must have overdone it!" he says out loud, and then gingerly works his way out of the gym and into the street.

Even with the street lights above the pavement, the area is dim, as the last speck of sun sets below the horizon. The further he goes the more lightheaded he becomes and he begins to feel as though one of the huge weights he was lifting earlier is resting on his chest. Paul is now struggling desperately to breathe and he finds himself overcome by tingling emotional spikes of paranoia and starts to believe he is being followed. "**Who's there**?" he calls out as his head swings frantically one way, then the other. The dark shadows of the posts are now swaying under the florescent spotlights as if they are dancing eerily to the beat of Paul's own heavy breathing. His clear and acute mind is now eclipsed with a nauseating haze that makes him want to throw up but he can't. Paul takes another swallow of his sports drink to rid himself of his dry mouth and the strange taste that regurgitates from the back of his throat, but instead of feeling better he's now feeling extremely ill and his light-headedness almost brings him to the point of collapse.

His instinct alerts him to the obvious. "The drink! It had to be the drink!" he slurs as he cups his hands over his eyes and rubs them vigorously. At this point he is doing all he can to remain conscious as his awareness is deteriorating rapidly and as he shakes his head from to side he loses his balance and almost falls, so he hunches over and balances himself by placing his hands upon his knees. "Pull it together, man!" he says to himself as desperation and overwhelming fear begins to set in. Like a prize fighter who is out on his feet, he continues his struggle but everything around him becomes distorted as he makes an effort to straighten up again. He staggers his way up the street like a drunk after an all-day session at the bar and the night becomes a blur of colourful lights that are smudged into shades of grey and pitch black. All of a sudden a van miraculously appears from nowhere and pulls over to the curb, so close its tyres rub on the embankment, emitting a screeching sound. All Paul can hear is a muffled voice echoing in and out of his head and as hard as he tries he can't keep his balance any longer and he topples while still semi-conscious, backward toward the pavement. Yet something behind him breaks his fall and that's the last thing he senses before complete unconsciousness.

As Paul slowly regains a vague semi-conscious state from his drug-induced sleep, he finds himself with a new nauseating discomfort and a frustrating haze covers his eyes like cellophane. He is now sitting upright and mobile with the sensation of being in the midst of a dream that lacks any clarity. There's no longer any sign of the blurred street lights or the sound of distant traffic, only darkness, the crackling of twigs and dried leaves below him and it's not long before his paranoia returns. Paul also hears a distorted heavy breathing of something behind him blended with the rustling of bushes as the cool evening breeze flutters through them. He desperately wants to shout out but he has nothing; he can only sit there shaking helplessly with the movement of the carriage supporting him. There is still no clearness of mind at this point, only instinct driving his will to survive. He tries desperately to adjust his vision by tiredly squinting but even the chilling cold breeze hitting his face is doing little to help his plight. It's almost the same sensation he felt when he was once on a drinking binge with his pals in the Special Forces only worse, much worse, his eyes are blurred and he feels saliva trickling down his chin. He attempts to wipe it but finds he can't move his wrists or legs. The sound of footsteps and breathing seem to be intertwining behind him and he wants to turn his head but it feels so heavy and there is something around his neck that is cold, thick and restraining any flexibility he has left.

The sky becomes slightly lighter as the moon momentarily eases its way out from behind a cloud and Paul can just make out the silhouette of a large building that seems to be moving like a drying towel in the wind.

As the drug continues to slowly breakdown in his system, he gains a little clarity and feels like he's riding on something but there's no sound of a motor, just a soft voice reverberating in his head; it sounds vaguely familiar but his mind is so absent from reality, it's difficult for him to be absolutely sure who it is.

"Well, I see you're on your way back to the real world."

Paul feels his carriage come to an abrupt halt almost in unison with the ceasing of the cool ghostly breeze that was whispering through the bushes. This creates a tense sharp silence but it also presents him with some relief from the drug induced paranoia, which sent his senses tingling each time he heard a bush shiver or a twig break. His relief is short-lived when the soft voice from earlier flows around him in confused sound waves, "I'll just leave you out here for a bit longer until we can be assured that you're fully alert when we begin the procedure." The voice's echo fades in and out of the still of the night, until there is an eerie silence, apart from the sound of his pulsating breath.

Paul then squints as a ghostly figure walks from behind his carriage and squats down at the front of him; all he can make out is the figure of a woman with short blond hair. Paul forcibly slurs his first words since the gym "Is that you, Kate?"

A contorted rapid reply reverberates back at him, "Of course, who else do you think it is? You will soon learn not to compare me to others!"

Paul tries hard to understand her meaning but the soft spoken voice continues to taunt him, "I just want you to know that you're not as special as you think you are and you're no different to all the others! So high and mighty, building me up and pretending you have feelings for me and then cutting my legs from under me. Do you know how much that hurts?"

Paul sits there silently, just staring directly and hypnotically at a blurred figure of a woman. He knows if he says anything at all it could only serve to inflame her emotions further. Beads of sweat run down his forehead and into his eyes and even when it stings like an ant bite, his special forces training has taught him to hold fast and show the enemy nothing. He's awoken from his trance like state when the shadowy figure screams at him, "**Well, do you**! No? Well you soon will!" The voice continues echoing through his head, like something he has only heard in his most frightening nightmares. A war rages within Paul as he becomes torn between the drug induced paranoia and the Special Forces training that lingers in his subconscious telling him to never to give in or give up.

"You've never really been cut down to size; have you Mr High and Mighty? Well, I'm looking forward to seeing you squirm like all those who went before you. Their eyes would bulge as they howled in terror. To some people this may seem horrific but to me it's dramatic and wonderful, just like a scene from an opera. So once that saw is halfway through, I'll listen and smile to the sound of your screaming. The others are no longer in control and nor will you be. When all's said and done, it will be me who decides when to end it, not you." Even with blurred vision, Paul gazes directly at his captor unflinchingly to remind the hazy figure standing in front of him that there will be no sadistic satisfaction received from his fear. The figure stands there in silence as if waiting for Paul to crack but soon realizes that he is much stronger willed than those that have gone before him, so the form switches on a flashlight, turns toward the barn and moves smoothly and quickly into the building.

It's not long after an almost inaudible, yet still recognisable sound of a chain passing over cogs and the muffled groan of something heavy being hoisted from its resting place fills Paul's mind with an unnerving curiosity. Gradually and in unison to the sound within, a stream of rectangular light slowly lurches its way forward out of the building and falling just short of where Paul sits awaiting his fate. Moments later, an eerie high pitched voice, musically flows from the barn, "Coming, ready or not" which would send bitter chills down the spine of even the most hardened men. Whatever it was that had been mixed in his drink earlier is now beginning to wear off and he can see a grey furtive form, materialising from the deep recesses of the barn while casting a long eerie shadow out and onto the open ground. The circulation in Paul's hands, fingers and feet has become so poor that even the pins and needles he felt earlier have turned to an uncomfortable numbness but that doesn't stop him from struggling to free them from the straps that hold him in their vice like grip. This ordeal has been a gruelling test of Paul's stamina, both physically and mentally; yet his will remains unbroken as he puts in a determined, super-human effort to break his bondage. Most others would have resigned themselves to what seems like a foregone conclusion but even with his brute strength, it has little impact on the leather straps that remain unyielding.

Just as the figure fully emerges and moves toward Paul, the barn illuminates from high powered lights hitting it and the surrounding area. Paul's instincts tell him it has to be his colleagues and it isn't long before his gut feeling is proven right. His heart warms further, when firm voices from the shrubs beyond the break echo out in the dark of night, ordering his captor to surrender, bringing a jarring end to Paul's isolated nightmare, "Are you okay, Paul?" Sebastian hollers with concern.

Paul's voice croaks back, "What do you think?"

There, in the glaring lights, stands a blonde who is forced to conceal blinded eyes behind a slender, horizontal, outstretched arm but like a startled rabbit inevitably decides to make a dash back inside. The assembled body of policemen move forward in a coordinated manner breaking the stillness of the night with rapidly moving boots and their demands for the culprit to halt but even the two burly policemen who merge from either side of the building can't grasp the nimble footed villain as the killer moves with shrewd athleticism, by rapidly shifting one way then the other and eventually disappearing into the cold dim recess of the barn. The officers wait cautiously outside with their pistols drawn, not knowing if the suspect they're pursuing is armed or not but they change their tactics when they hear a loud thud and the interior of the building turns pitch black. The two pursuers turn their high-powered torches on and slowly advance with apprehension into the depths of the darkness and after awhile they return empty handed with puzzled looks on their faces.

Charlie Betts, who is the officer in charge, has already read the faces of his two men leaving the barn and takes appropriate action. "Colin, Harry, take a couple of men with you and check the sides and back of the building for any trace of holes, doors or any other exits! Darren, Steve, guard the front of the barn and make sure no one comes out of there!"

Charlie stands back from the entrance with the rest of the group. The two officers who have searched the interior of the barn return to Charlie with their negative news. "There's no trace, Sir!"

Charlie's eyes light up. "What do you mean, there's no bloody trace, where is she?" he barks back at them.

"I don't know, Sergeant; we've searched every square inch of the interior but can't find anything. There are no gaps in the walls to squeeze through, nothing!" Charlie gives the go ahead for the other two officers guarding the entrance to go in and see if they can find the culprit but they come back empty handed as well.

Sebastian sees the dilemma the Police are having and strides briskly across the clearing to the Sergeant. "I think I can explain, Charlie." The Sergeant's brows come together like a hawk on the dive and his eyes are just as focused. "Someone better be able to, or I'm going to assume we're dealing with a bloody ghost!"

Sebastian puts his hand on the Charlie's shoulder, "No, nothing like that at all; without knowing what to look for or where to look for it, the hidden cellar is practically impregnable."

"Cellar? What cellar?"

"It's a long story but if you get one of your men to climb up the wooden ladder to the loft, and heave on the chain that dangles near it, he will find a trap door will open beneath him and a ramp will lead you down to where your culprit should be hiding. It is of the utmost importance that you tell your men to proceed with caution as the person they are seeking is extremely dangerous." The Sergeant gets one of the officers to open the trap door while a group of his peers move cautiously and silently down the ramp to the unknown below.

The moon eerily appears as the navy blue and purple clouds break their lock on its silver beams and Sebastian turns on his heels and lopes at a pace to where Paul sits helplessly bound and he quickly unbuckles the leather straps that bind him. "Don't move, Paul, 'til the ambulance gets here. It won't be long," Sebastian says in a concerned manner.

Paul smiles wearily but also proves to be headstrong and despite his discomfort his instinct is telling him to get to his feet; so he firmly pushes down on the sides of the wheelchair and Sebastian can see the intensive strain when his whole body begins to shake but as soon as he is upright he begins feebly struggling to maintain his balance and Sebastian helps him back into his seat. Paul, still feeling nauseous, finds Sebastian a comforting sight. He wearily looks up at him and huskily asks, "You wouldn't have something cold to drink, would you?"

Sebastian, with determined eyes and his cane held high, looks toward one of the policemen standing with the Sergeant and yells, "HO! YOU OVER THERE, CAN WE GET PAUL A DRINK?" he yells persuasively with his eyes thrashing from squinting lids. The Sergeant jolts his head to the side in Sebastian's direction to indicate to the officer to go ahead and the smaller fellow scurries over, passes an icy bottle into Sebastian's outstretched hand and Sebastian in turn holds the bottle out to Paul.

He shakily grasps and lifts the vessel with its liquid relief to his dry lips and swallows the soothingly cold stream down his raspy throat. "Shit, I needed that!" he croaks as the sound of ambulance sirens grow louder. They had been on standby and arrive minutes later.

Once Paul is taken away Sebastian squats down and is amazed at how ingeniously the old wheelchair had been converted into an instrument of restraint and torture to suit the killer's sadistic whims. He notices that the

131

wheels and footrests can be easily removed at any given time and the high neck and head rest is made of solid timber. The backrest and seat don't separate, making it simple for the victim to remain strapped in while being hoisted onto the operating bench. There is also an adjustable screw with a sharp end that penetrates through the neck rest, so if the victim were to push back with their head in order to avoid watching the procedure, the screw would ensure they couldn't.

Up until now Sebastian's senses hadn't been aroused by the gibbous moon or every time a bush rustled, as his concerns for Paul's safety had far outweighed any of his own fears, but he is now feeling he's seen enough and is becoming uncomfortable with his surrounds again, so he waits for one of the policemen to escort him back to the station. When no one comes to get him he becomes impatient and begins walking toward the Sergeant and two other officers who have emerged from the barn. The closer Sebastian gets to the group, the less he likes what he's hearing. "Yes, Sir, we did find the hidden room and we searched every inch of it but found nothing."

The Sergeant turns his head when he hears Sebastian's footsteps coming toward him. "Well, Seb, you must have heard what my officer just said; what do you make of it?"

A look of confusion comes over his face and although he really isn't in the frame of mind to enter the barn, Sebastian gets clearance to go in with the officer who has just come out. They take the steps down to the hidden cellar. "Shit, I must have missed something!" he states, frustrated, to the young officer in front of him.

"I don't know how you could have; we've searched every inch of the barn and the cellar without finding a thing."

Being intrigued by what he has missed, Sebastian stumbles and almost falls down the ramp and the young constable is quick to turn and catch hold of his arm. "Are you okay? We wouldn't want you hitting the hard concrete; you could end up breaking something!"

Sebastian thanks the officer, then taps his cane on the solid floor and turns to the accompanying officer with a sudden impulse. "Oh, yes! Of course! Why didn't I take notice of this before?"

The officer looks questioningly at Sebastian, "Sorry, am I missing something? What have you found?"

Sebastian lifts his eyes from his focus on the floor. "It's not what I have found but more about what I haven't found. As you can see, there is a hose over on the wall to clean up any residual blood but where does the water and blood flow to? There are no drain holes and there is certainly no bucket to remove it with. There has to be some way of the liquid escaping this room or we would be knee deep in it." Sebastian walks over to the wall and detaches the hose and turns it on full force. It's not long before water begins to build up. "There, over there, look!" Sebastian points toward bubbles coming from the wall opposite and farthest from the steps. "Behind there!" he proclaims in a conquering tone while pointing to a small wooden box against the wall. "That is where you will find what you are looking for."

"I don't mean to be rude but I doubt if our killer will fit into an old soap box, Sebastian," he replies sarcastically.

Sebastian walks over to the wooden box and pushes it away with his cane, then points to a lever that juts out of the wall and levels just below the top of the box when it is standing vertically. Below the lever is a vertical slit so the lever can be forced downward by the foot. "No, the culprit is not a gnome; the box is concealing the lever that opens the way out!"

He puts his foot on the top of the lever and pushes down hard and that in turn sets off a chain reaction; at the far end of the room the wall begins to lift exposing a dark narrow tunnel and at the other end of the room the hatch above the ramp where they entered from slams shut obliterating Sebastian's view of the steps leading out. Sebastian can see the escape tunnel is narrow and low and tells the policeman to go ahead while he waits in the cellar until the others come to let him out but unknown to him, they are all outside the barn searching the surrounding shrub and didn't hear the trap door close or notice the light go out. It seems like he is down there for an eternity, until he is finally released from his morbid dungeon and the officer who was with him explains that he followed the tunnel down the hill at the back of the barn until he reached a ladder leading up to another hatch. Once he climbed through the opening he found himself in shrub just off an old horse track that led to a dirt road further down. He went on to tell Sebastian that he could see there were tyre divots where a large car or van had ploughed off at considerable speed. He also explained that he had met up with a group of policemen who had heard dirt and gravel being hurled out from a vehicle and scurried down the old track but were far too late by the time they arrived at the dirt road. All that remained was a trail of dust where the perpetrator had sped off in haste. Sebastian has seen enough for one evening and arranges a lift back to the station.

Back to the station, he rings Cynthia. "Hello, my love. I'm sorry to tell you this but I'm going to be home quite late tonight."

Cynthia hesitates. "Did you catch the killer?"

"No, my love, I'm afraid we didn't, but I have a good idea who it is."

"Are you okay?"

Sebastian frowns and bites his bottom lip. "Yes, yes, I'm fine. But Paul has been whisked off to the hospital."

There's a moments silence. "Why, what happened? Is he okay?"

Sebastian moves quickly to negate any negative thoughts that Cynthia may have. "He's fine, my love, just fine and I'm heading over to see him now. They will probably keep him in overnight for observation, that's all."

After meeting Paul for the first time, Cynthia felt a bond as a mother would to her only son. "Why, was he shot? Tell me, what happened to him?"

"No, nothing like that. Seriously he is fine. I'm sorry my love but I have so much to do and I promise I will explain it all when I get home, alright?"

Cynthia, who is still sounding unconvinced, answers with some reservation, "Okay, but honestly, Sebastian, if you forget..."

Knowing what's about to be relayed to him, Sebastian jumps in quickly, "Don't worry, my love, I won't forget but I really must go now." He hangs up the phone and scurries up to Jim's office.

Emily has already gone so he goes straight to Jim's door and knocks. "Come in, Seb!" Jim calls in a very businesslike manner. Sebastian enters and Jim continues, "I just got a call through telling me our culprit got away; where to from here?"

Sebastian sits down in front of him. "Well, for a start, Jim, as soon as I leave here I will be driving to the hospital to see how Paul is and I was wondering if you would like to join me?"

Jim takes a deep breath and looks up at the ceiling, then back down at Sebastian with an apologising face. "Sorry, Seb. I did hear that Paul got caught up in this whole thing and, yes, I will go with you as I live only five minute's walk from the hospital. So that won't be a problem but, whichever way you look at it, we still have a serial killer on the loose!"

Sebastian pulls a notepad from his shirt pocket, rips out a page and hands it to Jim. "What's this?"Jim says through squinted eyes.

135

"If you can bring these people in for questioning tomorrow, I promise you I will deliver your serial killer before the day is out. But for now, I really must be getting over to the hospital; are you coming?"

Jim grabs his coat and hat and makes his way down to the car park with Sebastian and on the way over Jim makes numerous phone calls to several officers notifying them of who he wants to beplaced under surveillance for the evening and then to be brought in to be interviewed first thing the next morning. During the journey he looks at Sebastian and asks, "How do you know our killer won't skip town now the noose is tightening?"

Sebastian gives a sinister grin. "Because the killer has someone to remain for, someone they believe depends on them."

Jim and Sebastian eventually arrive at the hospital and sit with a very worn and drawn Paul who has just arrived back from his examination. Sebastian looks at him with concern. "How are you feeling, my friend?"

"Tired, Seb, but the doctor seems to think I'm in good shape and will have no side effects by morning apart from the possibility of a minor headache. They said it will be like having a hangover."

Jim is quick to add, "And a couple of days off won't hurt you, either."

Paul sits up and pushes his pillows vertical to support him. "Seriously, Jim, the Doc has given me the all clear to go back to work and I really need to do this."

Sebastian and Jim look at each other for a split second in silence and then Jim replies, "I want a certificate, do you understand?"

Paul smiles. "Thanks, boss, I appreciate that. Tell me, Seb... how did you know I would be there?"

"In all honesty, Paul, I didn't know **you** would be there but I knew someone would."

"After we had our first look at the barn, I was still a little curious about the new work that had been done on it, so I went back out for another look around yesterday after I had visited Joe Devonport's old neighbourhood and as soon as I arrived, I searched inside the building from top to bottom, looking for hatches, side doors or anything out of the ordinary. I knew there was more to the old barn than met the eye but I couldn't find any anomalies. So I took a stroll outside to clear my head and thought if I checked around the perimeter of the building, I may find some sort of concealed doorway but there was none."

"What I did find, though, was the length outside the barn seemed to differ from the inside, so I paced it out. In hindsight, I wish I'd focused more on the surrounding area and I probably would have found the track leading down to the road out the back. Anyway, I went back inside the barn and paced that out as well, only to discover it was three full strides shorter from front to back."

"So I began my search on the inside all over again, only this time I confined my observations to the rear of the building. I looked for scrape marks on the hard dirt floor where a door may have opened but there weren't any, nothing anywhere that would indicate a door or a latch. I got so frustrated I sat down on an old bale of hay, threw my head backward into my hands and stared at the roof. There dangling above me was a block and tackle used to hoist bales into the loft and my mind immediately cast back to the renovations we'd seen when we first went there. I asked myself what if the secret door doesn't swing in or out, what if it isn't on a hinge but slides upwards on a pulley system. I sprung to my feet and pulled on the chain but it was solid and had no give. So I climbed the ladder to the loft and used my cane to bring the chain and pulley over to me."

"There on the side of the pulley was a well-oiled latch which, once flicked back, freed the chain and allowed me to effortlessly haul down on it. I couldn't believe my eyes when the whole rear wall panel started to rise; in fact, the mechanism was so easy to operate a young child would have no problems getting it to work. I then realised the beam on the roof that held the hoist had been hollowed out and replaced with a metal compartment that contained an array of pulleys and cables which in turn was duplicated on the side beam and connected to the rear wall."

"Once the door was lifted I found a large hatch which connected to the same system and opened in unison. A ramp led down into a concealed cellar confirming my initial thoughts about the tyre tracks you found. They were very faint and difficult for me to see, so I put my penknife across the breadth of the tyre imprints; that way I could look across either end of the knife and calculate if there was a coinciding track and, of course, there was. That is what led me to believe these were tyre tracks from a wheelchair and, of course, this made a lot of sense if the killer was acting on their own. You see, if the culprit was of slight build, the chair would make a limp body manageable. My biggest mistake was to assume that the only way someone would bring a wheelchair to the barn would be from the main road and that was my downfall when it came to capturing the killer this evening. It's possible that the cellar may have been built as a bomb shelter during the Cold War or may even date back further."

"The room below contains a diesel driven generator that's used for driving the electric saw and also a pump that draws the water from the creek. Now, listen to me! I can see that you are tired and on the way over we organised a meeting for ten o'clock tomorrow when I will explain a few more things. So we will leave you for now and I will pick you up at nine-thirty sharp. Did you want me to notify anyone? Chelsea or your mother, perhaps?"

Paul slowly moves his head from one side of the pillow to the other. "No. Better not, Seb. My mother will only panic and Chelsea will leave an important photo shoot to come home; I'll let them know in good time but I would appreciate it if you could pick me up a change of clothes for the morning; the keys to my apartment are in my trouser's pocket," he mutters drowsily and then smiles wearily.

Sebastian grabs the keys and he and Jim say their farewells; once outside Jim whips his head toward a café on the corner. "Would you like a coffee before you head home, Seb?"

Sebastian's hand goes up showing his palm. "No thanks, Jim. I have to get home. It's been a big day and it's going to be a bigger one tomorrow."

Jim looks Sebastian earnestly in the eyes. "Tell me, Seb. Do you honestly believe Paul is ready to come back tomorrow?"

Sebastian closes his eyes and nods gently. "If the doctor has given him the all clear, then from my perspective as a psychologist it would be the best possible thing for him to do. He has been through a hell of an ordeal tonight and being able to not only face the person who did this to him but also to put the predator away for life will hand him back control of the situation and should also bring him closure. On the other hand, if he can't watch the unravelling of this cold blooded killer, then all his subconscious is left with is the nightmare of tonight."

Jim slips his hands in his jacket pockets as a chilly breeze whips up. "That makes perfect sense, Seb. I better let you go and I will catch up with you and Paul in the morning."

Sebastian works his way through the car park to his car and with his mind filled with the events of the day, it seems like his half hour drive has passed in minutes as he pulls into the driveway of his home. The front porch light is on and Cynthia opens the door to greet him as soon as she hears him motoring down their drive. Before he can even get out of the car she gracefully glides across the veranda and waits outside his car door with her arms crossed to keep out the bitter cold. Sebastian clumsily works his way out of the driver's seat and she kisses him, hugs one of his arms and walks in with him while still attached.

"Put your coat and cane up and then go to the study. There's bourbon in there, just waiting for you to enjoy, and once you have finished it, come join me in the kitchen. I kept dinner back so we can sit down and discuss the events as they unfolded."

Sebastian obediently does exactly what Cynthia has requested of him and then relates the whole day's events to her over dinner. Cynthia is more than relieved to hear that Paul is okay. By the end of dinner, she can see that Sebastian is physically and mentally exhausted so she talks him into having an early night.

The following morning Sebastian is up early and drives to Paul's apartment to pick up some fresh clothes and then motors to the hospital to get Paul at nine thirty sharp. "Good morning, my friend. Now here are your clothes but more importantly… how are you feeling?"Sebastian asks sincerely while handing Paul his attire.

Paul looks much livelier than he did the previous night, so he immediately takes his clothes into the change room and returns a muffled reply, "I'm feeling much better than I did last night, Seb, and if you go to the drawer in the side table next to the bed, you will find the signed release form from my doctor." Paul comes out of the change room still doing up his belt and Sebastian gives him the papers he has retrieved from the drawer. "I'm ready to go when you are, Seb, "he says with a grin from ear to ear and they make their way to the registrar where he signs out.

Once they are in the car and heading toward the station, Sebastian is so enthusiastic about having Paul back he doesn't stop talking all the way. He fills Paul in on his visit to Joe Devonport's old neighbourhood and even a few of his own personal trials and tribulations.

Sebastian parks the car and the two of them make their way up the steps of the building. When they get inside and begin to work their way through the hordes of police officers and detectives, there are constant words of encouragement and pats on the backs for Paul.

Sebastian looks at him proudly. "You deserve this, my friend. You are a very brave man."

Paul is humbled by his words. "Thanks, Seb. That means a lot to me!"

Sebastian looks him in the eyes and smiles. "Yes, I know. Now, I would like you to go ahead of me as there is something I need to attend to. I won't be long." Before Paul has an opportunity to respond Sebastian has left, so he continues on his way to Jim's office and no sooner has he entered, Emily walks around the desk to hug him. "How are you, Paul… and do you really think you should be here?"

Paul looks at her gratefully. "I'm fine, Emily, and I don't think it's a matter of wanting to be here; I think I have to be here. You know that old thing about getting back on the horse?"

Emily closes her eyes and nods. "Yes, I think I know what you mean; anyway Jim is expecting you two, so where is your other half?" Paul looks down, tightens his lips and waves his head from side to side and Emily's empathic look soon turns to a stern glare. "Well he better get here soon, as Jim's patience won't remain passive forever, you know!"

Paul is about to stall a little longer when Sebastian enters the room and is slightly out of breath. "Sorry...had something to do...that just had to be done..." Emily holds her index finger vertically in front of her face and glares at Sebastian, then moves to Jim's door and announces them.

The first thing Paul does is hand over the hospital clearance forms to Jim and then they both take a seat. "Good to see you here in one piece, Paul. How are you feeling?"

"Good thanks, Jim. After you guys left I slept like a baby; maybe I should do this sort of thing more often!" he says with a smile.

Jim grins for a small moment and then takes on a more serious persona. "Okay, Seb, give us a rundown of what's unfolding here. I can't hold these people forever, you know!"

Sebastian sits back with his arms crossed. "We will get to them shortly, Jim, and it shouldn't take that long."

Sebastian switches his attention to Paul. "Now, Paul, you may recall me saying at one of our meetings it seemed to me to be too coincidental and convenient that each time a murder was committed, Kate was away on some sort of junket. After seeing and talking to her, I found her to be the type of person who would find it more productive working at her business, rather than being overseas attending seminars that would show nothing more than she already knows."

"When I requested Cynthia to ring the hotel where Kate had supposedly stayed on a previous trip, I asked her to inform the clerk that she was a friend of Kate's and that Kate had recommended the hotel to her. Fortunately, the clerk knew Kate very well and loved a good chat while he wasn't busy. During their conversation he mentioned Kate's son who has cerebral palsy."

Paul chips in, "She's got a son?"

Sebastian screws up the corner of his mouth in a chastising way. "Let me finish, Paul! "Anyway, when Cynthia heard this, alarm bells began going off, as they just did with you, my friend. I had filled Cynthia in on my progress the night before and as you know Kate had informed everyone that she had no family; so you can understand why Cynthia delved even further. She made a very clever decision to ring the airport and find out what name the tickets for Kate's previous flight had been booked under and, sure enough, she was travelling with a young boy by the name of Dylan McConkey. Because the boy's name is so rare, Cynthia said it wasn't hard to trace the mother of the child and – surprise, surprise – both the mother, whose real name is Michelle and her son Dylan live in an apartment owned by Kate. I kept asking myself why Kate would take this other woman's child on trips with her but the biggest problem I had was when I called to see Michelle she wasn't there, so I rang Cynthia to do some more probing and she rapidly found the child's grandparents."

Sebastian turns to Paul and then continues, "I also rang Jim and asked him to send someone to the airport to detain Kate so I could speak to her after I had spoken to Michelle. When I eventually called to see Michelle's parents, they were more than happy to tell me how they cast her out after she fell pregnant and her no good boyfriend – whose name just happened to be Nathan Spedding – had blown town."

Jim slumps back in his chair and places his fingertips on the edge of his desk. "Are you kidding me? Are you talking about the same Nathan Spedding who is on our list of victims?"

Sebastian closes his eyes and gently nods his head in the affirmative. "Yes, Jim. With all that's been going on I haven't had the opportunity to explain that to you and, as strange as this all sounds, it is the very same one. Anyhow, Michelle's parents went onto tell me she was adopted by them and that they had a choice of taking both identical twins. The McConkeys only wanted one and they believed they'd chosen the wrong child. When Michelle was brought back from the airport so I could interview her, she seemed reluctant to speak up but after finding out she was now involved in a murder investigation, she explained to me she was actually Michelle and not Kate. Once I told her what had happened to Nathan Spedding, she had no hesitation in admitting she had impersonated her sister on the overseas trips and was only too happy to cooperate."

Paul looks at Sebastian curiously. "But how did you know Kate was flying out yesterday?"

"I tried to contact Kate at the gym and I was told by Max she was having a few days off to attend a seminar overseas; so I simply rang the airport and found out there had been a flight booked by Kate for that very day. I tried to contact you but you didn't answer."

He looks at Paul whose mouth opens wide as he glances up to the ceiling and then back to Sebastian. "Damn battery went dead in my phone."

Sebastian hangs his head and swings it from side to side. "I had no idea that you would be the next victim. All I knew was each time the victims were killed, Kate's plane had taken off that day and what better alibi than to be in mid-flight when a murder is committed. I was desperate and determined to stop this killer striking again so I called Jim and ..."

Jim interrupts, "I organised for Seb and a group of well-trained men to be dropped off at the bottom of the drive..."

Sebastian cuts back in again, "And we hiked our way up to the barn for the stakeout. I felt the only way to connect the murderer to the barn was to be there during the time of the abduction, so there we were. The unmarked cars that dropped us off went back down to the highway and parked in well concealed positions awaiting our signal if the culprit should be good enough to get past us. As you and I discovered when we first went there, the road at the end of the driveway could only be accessed via the highway."

"I knew that the victim wouldn't be overdosed, as they would need to suffer for emotionally hurting her. I am so angry with myself for not realising you would be the next victim, as I should have been aware that you would have to be high on the agenda because of the close connection you had with Kate. The other thing I didn't count on was the hidden back entrance but by the time we were in position, it was too late to change the way things were set up and we were all surprised in more ways than one when the two of you emerged from behind the barn and not the route we had expected. The important thing is you're safe and it won't be long before we have our murderer well and truly behind bars. Now, Paul, would you like to join me in Interview Room One?"

Paul and Sebastian rise from their seats in unison. "Wouldn't miss it for the world, Seb," Paul says eagerly.

"Now, listen, you two. I want a full report on my desk by the end of the day and I also want this killer behind bars!" Jim states with authority as the two of them leave the room and work their way down toward their first interview.

As they are strolling down the hallway Paul glances across at Sebastian. "We haven't talked much about that Joe Devonport character, Seb. After what you told me on the way here about him, surely there's a possibility he has had some involvement in this whole thing?"

Sebastian smiles at Paul then replies proudly, "That is exceptional logic, Paul; his profile does fit that of a serial killer but there are also others who don't fit the profile, yet have a motive."

Paul's brow folds. "So, are you saying he is innocent?" he asks inquisitively.

"No, Paul. I'm not saying he is innocent; I am simply saying that there are others to be considered and some things aren't always what they seem." The two men stop outside the first interview room and Sebastian holds the handle to the door. "Are you ready?" Paul tightens his lips with an acknowledging grin and nods his head in the affirmative.

As they enter for the first interview, Paul looks sternly across to a sad face sitting timidly behind the desk and Sebastian takes a seat while he remains standing at the rear of the room. "Sorry to keep you so long; the gentleman behind me is..."

Paul's lips tighten. "She knows who I am; she just didn't know I worked for the police!"

Sebastian throws his left arm over the back of his chair as he turns to look at Paul. "No, Paul, you are very wrong! She has no idea who you are; this is Michelle, Kate's identical twin sister."

"You're kidding me, Seb!"

Sebastian smiles at Paul and replies, "Not at all, Paul. That's why they are called identical twins." Sebastian swings back around, while Paul squints across at Michelle in amazement. "Okay, Michelle, we have had a brief discussion but I just need to clear a few more things up, if that is alright with you?"

Michelle, now looking extremely anxious and with pathetic eyes, she gazes across the desk at Sebastian and then over to Paul when answering. "I guess so." Her hands are clasped tightly, to the point where her knuckles are turning white.

Sebastian shifts his seat forward which makes a scraping noise on the floor and draws her attention back to him. "Alright then... perhaps you would like to tell me how you came into contact with Nathan Spedding after years of absence?"

Michelle's fingers shake as she rubs her brow nervously and her eyes glance mournfully downward. "I was at the airport with Dylan on one of my trips overseas. Kate told me she liked to have time to catch up on paperwork and she said that if she shut up the shop without a reasonable excuse, customers at the gym would complain. She also told me it was nice to be able to treat Dylan and me away for a break and when I said I was concerned about the expense, she told me not to worry as she could claim it on tax benefits anyway."

Sebastian looks strongly into her eyes. "So, tell me what happened when you ran into Mr Spedding at the airport?

Michelle looks at Sebastian with a folded frown and resistance in her eyes. "At first I didn't recognise him, as he had aged and grown a beard, but he knew who I was and seemed overjoyed to see me. He told me he had never married and felt bad about abandoning us. He said he had searched for us to no avail and it may seem crazy but I actually believed him. I have cared for my son for so long I haven't had time to have another man in my life but this was different, this was the father of my son and my first love.

So I began seeing him secretly after that but as time passed he wanted more. He wanted our relationship out in the open and he just wouldn't let up until we had a huge argument. He wanted me to tell Kate so there would be no more secrets but I just couldn't. I know now I was wrong but the reason I didn't want Kate to know was she had been a rock to both me and Dylan and I felt that Nathan and I hadn't been seeing each other long enough to be sure that he wasn't going to leave us stranded again. When Nathan never came back after the argument, I assumed I was right about him and he had just walked out on us the same way he did the last time. But you proved that theory wrong didn't you!"

Sebastian rises to his feet. "Thank you for your patience, Michelle. Now, if you can spare me a little more of your time, I would like you to wait here while we interview your sister; if you don't mind, of course."

She looks at Sebastian inquisitively. "I have told you all I know; why are you detaining me?" she says impatiently.

Sebastian shows no emotion when he replies, "No one is detaining you and you may leave now but it does seem strange that you don't want to know who killed Nathan, doesn't it?"

Michelle's face takes on a stern look, "I already know who killed Nathan; it had to be my sister. What more is there to know?"

"It's plausible that your sister did kill him but is it probable? I'm not sure yet. Oh, by the way, how can we be sure you were on all of those plane flights and not your sister?"

Her eyes bounce from one side to the other at a rapid pace. "How could I have been in two places at the same time? You know where I was... and anyway, you had me detained at the airport yesterday so that proves I was going on those trips!"

Sebastian looks deep into her nervous eyes. "It proves you were boarding a plane yesterday but it doesn't prove you were on the flight when Nathan was murdered. Now, would you mind waiting for a little while longer, please?"

Michelle, now looking incredibly uncomfortable, replies, "I would prefer not to but I agree it will be interesting to see who killed him." Sebastian and Paul leave the room and walk down the corridor to the next interview room.

++++

As Sebastian and Paul enter the interview room they find Kate sitting on the far side of the desk, leaning forward with her head resting on her crossed arms. The sound of the door opening brings her to attention and her disappointed eyes immediately catch Paul off guard making him feel slightly uncomfortable and creating an awkward silence, yet he still manages to return a glance back at her which is filled with unspoken questions. Sebastian takes a seat opposite, while Paul, as before remains standing by the door like a sentinel.

Sebastian slumps back into the chair, supports his right elbow with his left hand and begins gently pinching his bottom lip. "Hello, Kate. I would assume by now you have been filled in as to why you are here," Sebastian says as he readies himself to scrutinize every word and body movement she is about to make.

"Yes, I have been, but everything I've done can be explained," she says with some contempt. Paul remains quiet but his eyes bounce up and down from the ceiling and his facial expressions are blatantly obvious to what he is thinking. Kate's quick to notice this and her annoyed look now turns to anger as she senses his doubts. "I wasn't lying when I told you that my father drowned and that my mother had passed away from cancer when I was nineteen. I just chose not to tell you that before my mother died, she let me know that I'd been adopted."

"After some years of research to find my biological parents, I learnt I had an identical twin sister and the reasons for our adoption. I was deeply hurt to find out that our mother had placed us in an orphanage and then suicided six months later after the man that impregnated her ran off with another woman. What devastated me further was when I finally found him living at the farm house on his own; he informed me he had told her that he never wanted anything to do with me or my sister. Do you know what he said then?"

Sebastian still remains emotionless and answers, "No. What?"

"He looked at me with eyes that were as dead as the coldest corpse and said he had told my mother 'if she didn't get rid of us, he was finished with her.' Can you believe that stupid woman chose him over my sister and me? And then that bastard left anyway! Exactly six months after she adopted us out, she was found dead in her bath with both her wrists slit. As far as I'm concerned the day she put us in that orphanage, she did us both a big favour anyway. If she had decided to give us up under those circumstances, then who knows what would have happened if she'd kept us."

"I'd heard enough from my so called father and that's the last time I remember tears flowing down my cheeks. I told him I hated him and he stood there, towering over me, telling me to get the fuck off his property. He said I was a pathetic, weeping, little moron like my mother and then spat on me. Enough was enough, something snapped inside of me like a rigid twig. As much as I wanted to belong, I knew if I didn't walk away and start a new life, I would end up bitter and twisted like him and her, so I left and never saw him or the property again!" she says with a lamentable look now veiling her face.

147

Sebastian isn't about to ease up on her; he leans closer toward the table and stares accusingly and directly into her eyes

"If it is as you say it is, perhaps you can explain to me how you obtained your father's property after his death?"

Kate's face screws up as she slumps back into the chair and her head begins slowly swaying from one side to the other. "Are you kidding me? What the hell are you talking about?"

Sebastian's determined not to remove his piercing eyes from hers. "I assure you, this is no laughing matter. Come on, Kate! You need to give us the truth."

Kate crosses her arms on the table and her eyes flicker around like a moth in a light. "I am telling you the truth; I never bought that bastard's land. Why the hell would I want it?"

"I don't know. You tell me! We have been in touch with the local shire and you were listed as the property owner up until you sold the farm to Mike Cohen, which was just before his demise. Did he find out about the secret cellar?" he says as his glassy eyes continue to scan her every movement.

"No! What, what secret cellar? I still have no idea what you're talking about. I never purchased my so-calledfather's property; I never saw him after that day!" she replies in a panicked state.

Sebastian continues relentlessly, "We also know you were familiar with a fellow by the name of Nathan Spedding who had a close connection to your sister and that you and he had a fall out as well. Is that true?"

Her panic quickly turns to anger. "Yes, I knew about Michelle and that weasel Spedding. At first, I had no idea who he was, just another salesman who had come into my shop from time to time trying to get me to buy something I didn't need. I only put up with it because he would buy the odd drink off me but he would always be asking questions!"

Sebastian curiously asks, "Like what?" and she continues, "Mostly about family: things like 'did I have a big family or any siblings?' Then one day he approached me in an angry mood and started raising his voice in my shop, telling me I was holding my sister back. And when I asked him who the hell he was, he told me, so I told him to get out of my shop and never come back. He said he never wanted to set eyes on my sister or me again. Why? Did he have something to do with these murders? Because it wouldn't surprise me!"

Sebastian ignores her question and continues, "Did you tell your sister what happened?"

Kate swallows and exhales heavily through her nose. "What would be the point? It would only make her unhappy and cause problems between the both of us, so I just left it at that."

Sebastian probes again, "Did anyone else hear the argument?"

Kate tilts her head slightly and then glares upward. "They could have but not as far as I'm aware. There was no one else in the shop at the time."

Sebastian leans forward further, places his elbows on the desk while intertwining his fingers and then rests his chin on his knuckles. "So you didn't know that Nathan Spedding was murdered not long after your somewhat heated debate?"

Kate's jaw drops and her eyes bulge unnaturally. "No, of course I didn't know; how the hell would I?"

Sebastian slumps back into the seat again while crossing his arms. "Well, you tell me! Just give us someone who may have seen you or been with you when these murders took place."

Kate's head flops down and then rises just as quickly. "You know I can't because, when my sister took my place on the trips overseas, I stayed home, did my bookwork and kept to myself." A determined look washes over Kate's face. "Look, it might be time I called my lawyer!" Then she snaps her attention in the direction of Paul and says, "In all honesty, Paul, I really don't give a shit whether you believe me or not. I didn't kill either one of those sons of bitches and I didn't have anything to do with buying that low life's land. I feel bad about Spedding for my sister's sake but whoever killed the mongrel that sired us deserves a big pat on the back.

Paul curves up the corner of his mouth in frustration and says, "Come on, Kate! All the evidence points your way. Who do you think you're..?"

Sebastian swings his legs to the side of the chair and places his left arm over the backrest so he is looking directly at Paul and then quickly intervenes, "No, Paul. It's possible you were right all along; she may be telling the truth. Our killer is waiting down the hall for us."

Paul's eyes literally bulge from their sockets and he glares down at Sebastian with rage. "What are you talking about, Seb? If what you're saying is true, then what the hell are we doing here?"

"Sorry, Paul. I just wanted to be sure she was telling the truth and I am now reasonably convinced she is. I felt it necessary for you to hear what Kate had to say as you held faith in her from the beginning."

Kate, who has buried her face in her hands, slowly lifts her head. "Is that true, Paul? You actually believed all along that I wasn't the killer?"

Paul gently lifts his eyes back toward Kate. "Yes, it is. But there was a point where I was allowing my belief in you to override my police work and that's not a good thing."

Sebastian rises from his seat, moves toward the door and puts his hand on Paul's shoulder. "Come on, my friend. We have one last port of call before we throw our killer behind bars. I would like you to wait here a little longer, Kate, if you don't mind. Would you like a coffee or something to eat?"

"No, I'm fine. Thanks."

Sebastian gives her a gaze that has moved beyond any initial interest. "Thank you for your patience; hopefully you won't be here too much longer," he replies in a nonchalant manner.

++++

Once out in the corridor, Paul's curiosity gets the better of him. "What now, Seb?"

Sebastian grins confidently and waves his head to follow him. "Well, let's see where this all leads us. But before we go... how are you holding up?"

"I'm doing okay. Seb. I think the only thing that is bothering me at the moment is my curiosity." They move to a room further down.

"Well, Paul, I am hoping this brings our case to a climax and puts the killer behind bars," Sebastian says, as he holds the handle to the door that they are about to enter through. Paul stands there silently but gives Sebastian a few positive short nods and they proceed into the room. On entry, Sebastian moves forward to towards the seat at the desk in front of him, while Paul takes his position by the door and his face becomes eclipsed with confusion. Before Sebastian sits down he looks back at Paul to make sure he is okay and then directly back into the dead eyes of the culprit sitting in front of him."I hope we haven't kept you too long."

An unanimated figures its silently with eyes that lead to nowhere yet, from time to time, slowly and deliberately swap from Sebastian to Paul in a calculating manner. Sebastian takes his seat and continues, "So, before we start our questions, perhaps I should explain why you are here and how I knew you were involved in several murders. The one thing you may not be aware of but really should know is that Kate Kensington has a twin sister."

Joe Devonport's brows meet and his eyes come to life. Sebastian continues with determination, "Yes, I can see by your expression that my statement has taken you by surprise. Well, let us see if I can continue to amaze you with what I know." Sebastian says arrogantly while watching Joe's eyes and body movements. "Michelle, who is Kate's identical twin, had a baby on her sixteenth birthday and the father, also a sixteen-year-old, had run away from home after finding out Michelle had fallen pregnant. She barely coped through her teenage years and when she reached adulthood, she struggled to pay her rent. So you can imagine that there was simply no way she could afford a car with a hoist for the rickety old chair that had been donated to her and her son by a local charity group."

"In the meantime, Kate had been informed that she had a sister and searched diligently until she eventually found her. This was all the family Kate had left and she wanted to make sure her sister and nephew were well catered for, so she set her up in a unit and bought her a van with a hoist and a new wheelchair."

Joe finally breaks his silence with a sneer. "That's a lovely story," he says smugly and follows it up with, "So what's all that crap got to do with me?"

Sebastian is aware he has opened communication with his story and arrogant approach, so he continues, "I will let you know when I feel it's time for you to comment but in the meantime, I would prefer if you remained silent while I continue; even though I don't believe someone of your lesser standard deserves an answer to that ridiculous question, I will attempt to give you one anyway."

The whites of Joe's eyes become apparent and he glares with rage at Sebastian as he continues. "Kate's sister Michelle has nothing to do with you but her son's old wheelchair does. Now we all know you have a small van and work for Kate delivering boxes of her Kate Energy to other gyms; so when the workload became tedious, Kate asked you if you could convert an old wheelchair into a type of trolley to help you unload and load the boxes from your van. She probably told you that it was her mother's so she could keep her little secret hidden but the fact of the matter is you didn't only convert the chair into a workable trolley for your deliveries; you also adapted it to help you with your sinister deeds. Last night it was almost impossible to recognise you at the barn, when you were dressed in a cheap copy of Kate's clothing and a blonde wig but the one clue that would tie you to these hideous murders was that wheelchair."

Sebastian looks over his shoulder at Paul. "On my way in this morning, before I picked you up, I gave Charlie Betts a call and asked if he could show Michelle the chair before I arrived and see if she could identify it; apparently she had no problems at all, as she had engraved her son's initials under one of the arms of the chair where it could not be seen. If you recall, my friend, I popped out for a short while before our meeting. I did this so I could get the confirmation first hand from Michelle. She told me she had always had a terrible fear of the chair being stolen, as she had been living in some very shady areas, so she wanted some way of identifying it, if ever it was. Now, Paul, perhaps you have a question you would like to ask Mr Devonport?" Sebastian says, in the hope that a question coming from someone who Joe was incapable of emotionally conquering, will send him over the edge.

Paul glares across the room with fire in his eyes. "I only have one question for you...**why**?"

Joe Devonport's eyes penetrate Paul's like a savage dog that's about to bite and he can no longer hold back the twisted evil that reigns within. "You **truly** are a **fool,** aren't you? Just like **you**, those other miserable animals needed to be taught a lesson and **then** put down. Kate Kensington is a goddess and should be treated that way! I was put on this earth to unite and take care of her; she needs protecting from slimy scum like **you**! It wasn't hard to figure you for a cop, suddenly appearing out of the blue, right after Mike's execution. I could have ignored your snooping around, as **pigs** of your kind do but when I saw Kate's eyes light up when you were around her and the way she walked on air when she strolled up to meet you at the coffee shop that morning, I knew it could only end in disappointment for her, so I had to take care of things the way I always have. **You didn't know that, did you pig**? You had no idea I was there watching your every move," he says with a curled lip and a chuckling tone.

Paul's eyes are unmoving and fearless but he is finding it almost impossible to refrain from dragging Joe across the table and throttling him. If it wasn't for his training and Sebastian's guidance, he may have done so but for now he stands silently with his arms crossed while his mentor scrutinises and matches wits with this psychopath.

Sebastian is aware of the tension building in the room and immediately changes tactics. "Tell us about Nathan Spedding," Sebastian says with meaning.

Joe is still breathing deeply from his rant and his eyes haven't shifted from Paul's. He curls one side of his lip, flicks his head up at Paul and then looks directly across the desk to Sebastian. "All I know is every time he came into the shop when I was there; he made Kate feel uncomfortable with his probing questions about her family. Then one day I was about to enter her shop and I heard him screaming at her, so I hid to the side where they couldn't see me."

"Did you hear what was being said?"

"I only arrived at the end of it all and he said 'the both of you can get fucked, you won't be seeing me again'. I waited awhile and then walked in to see Kate wiping away tears. I asked if she was okay and she just asked me to give her some time alone. That **Mister** High and Mighty Spedding wasn't walking away so easily; in fact, he didn't walk away at all. Isn't it amazing how an attitude can change when a superior takes control? At least, he met his maker humbly and not with the same contempt he showed when he was talking down to her!"

"We also know Owen Coleman came to grief in the same way; I gather this is your handy work as well?"

Joe pulls against the cuffs as he opens his hands and a large smile eclipses his face. "Well, what can I say? You've either got it or you haven't."

Sebastian keeps a straight face. "Sometimes it's easy for someone to brag about other people's achievements, and who knows...perhaps you are just a copycat killer who admired someone else's good work?"

The smile immediately leaves Joe's face and his eyes become lifeless and haunting. "I copy no man and no man will ever copy me! He was just another pathetic mortal who played a game with Kate's emotions and ended up the loser. The filthy pig was married and it broke her heart when she found out. She broke down and cried on my shoulder while telling me about this despicable cretin. He not only had to pay for what he did to my Kate but also what he did to his wife as well. I didn't have to copy anyone and once your men are done searching my home – which I'm sure they will be doing as we speak – they will come across a letter of apology to both Kate and his wife. He was only too happy to write it when he saw the blade closing in on his precious legs. I guess he thought I would release him once it was signed but people like him only go back to their indecent nature, so I showed him that this world has no tolerance or place for that sort of behaviour," he boasts with lurid details.

Sebastian sighs deeply as he shuts his eyes and his brow folds. "Just one more question, Joe?" he says enquiringly.

Joe looks up as if he's someone of importance answering questions for enquiring minds. "Sure go ahead! Why not?"

Sebastian leans forward. "Do you know anything about Kate's father's death? I'm assuming it was an accident as it's unlike anything you have done so far."

Joe pulls a tight-lipped smile, gives an icy stare and then gives out an immensely sinister chuckle. "Maybe I do or maybe I don't or maybe you need to find out for yourself. Either way, I've said enough, so go fuck yourself!"

Sebastian waves his head from side to side in disgust, which brings a broad smile to the maniac's face. Sebastian knows he has to find a flaw in Joe's cold calculating manner and his goal is to question, probe and antagonise him until he finds the Achille's heel that will open the lock to the unanswered questions that lie within this psychopath's inner sanctum; so he rises from his chair, turns and looks at Paul. "Can I have a word with you outside please, Paul?"

Paul blankly stares back at Sebastian in a way that says 'what for?' but knows better than to question his partner. "Uh, yes; okay, Seb."

Sebastian turns back to face Joe with calculating eyes and comments in his most clinical voice, "We won't be a moment."

Joe glares back with a sarcastic childlike sneer on his face and replies, "Take your time. I'm not going anywhere," and then begins laughing at his own little joke.

Once outside, Paul and Sebastian peer back through the observation window at Joe and he sits there revelling in his solitude while smugly smiling.

His eyes reveal that all humanity has perished from the depths of his soul and a more sinister identity now inhabits the void. Paul turns his head toward Sebastian and keenly asks, "What's going on, Seb?"

As Sebastian glances back, the all-knowing and confident face that he normally wears has faded into a thoughtful and doubtful expression. "I know this is unlike me but I have a hunch that he may have had something to do with Kate's father's death as well. I would like to use her as a psychological trigger to get him to admit his guilt, if it's okay with you?"

Paul, surprised by Sebastian's candour, responds, "Sure, Seb. Sure."

So they return back into the interview room and Joe begins waving his head from side to side with his eyes pointing to the ceiling. "What took you fools so long; I was getting lonely," he smirks and is highly amused by his own comments.

Sebastian isn't, and suppresses his temptation of showing his rage. He feels it's time to turn the tables and put a stop to Joe's cocky frivolity. "To be honest, I don't think there is anything else we need from you, Joe. We have enough to send you away for a long time. Are you ready, Paul? We need to get back and wrap up the case against Kate."

Immediately after Sebastian's comments a squint of mistrust appears in Joe's eyes; then his eyes race past Sebastian to Paul who is about to open the door and then back to Sebastian who disengages from the interview. Sebastian stands, turns and begins to walk toward the doorway but before he gets far, a half grinning and extremely nervous Joe with a folded brow responds with a new sharpness in his voice, "Hold on a minute, what are you talking about? What's going on with Kate?"

Sebastian turns side on and glances back over his shoulder in a nonchalant manner. "I really don't have time for this but if you have to know, Paul and I are about to head into the interview room next door and charge Kate with the murder of her father. We know she bought the property after he was killed, probably as some sort of trophy and once she had no more use for it, she sold it off to Mike Cohen. I'm sure if we exhume her father's body, we will find the cause of his death wasn't due to a fall which knocked him unconscious prior to burning to death as initially suspected but it is more likely he was given a concoction that would have rendered him unconscious. With the equipment the Coroner has these days it shouldn't be too hard to find traces of whatever drug was used, still in his remains, "Sebastian explains persuasively.

Joe's eyes burn like hot needles into Sebastian's as he sharply raises his attention to his remarks; the lack of interest has turned to an uneasy arousal and the sneering smile he was wearing has now parted from his face as he continues to cast his venomous glare in Sebastian's direction. Sebastian remains standing silently with a wry, baiting grin set like cement on his face and his eyes confidently focus back at Joe's. There is no doubt in Sebastian's mind he has found Joe's Achille's heel as he can see he can't contain his rage any longer. Joe rises to his feet, clenches his fists, slams them on the table and loses his intent to hold back. "You dirty fucking low life, you fucking scum! I'll fucking kill you before you hurt her in any way! Fuck you!"

Paul steps forward to protect his partner. "Sit down, Joe, or do I have to shackle you?"

Joe sees the seriousness in Paul's eyes and immediately takes a seat. "Fuck you!" he says while staring daggers at Paul.

At this point, Sebastian's confidence glows sarcastically on his face and Joe's bold tirades only lead to fuelling Sebastian's fire further. "You won't be killing anyone where you're going and you certainly won't be able to stop us sending her to prison as well. I outsmarted you and I've outsmarted her as well!"

Joe's confident face becomes filled with annoyance, he slams his fists on the table again and then glares across the room at Sebastian so intensely, his eyes bulge a convex white from their sockets. His intent to withhold information becomes impossible for him and he becomes angrily garrulous. "Oh yes, you're the man! You're so fucking clever... you couldn't even work out that she didn't buy the property; I bought it in her name."

Sebastian places his hands on the back of his empty seat and he smirks, "Who signed the original papers then?"

"Me, of course; I've made enough deliveries to her shop to be able to forge her signature with my eyes shut but before I did that, I took out an additional loan on my own home to pay for it. Real estate agents don't really care who is representing their buyers, as long as the cash is on the table; so once I took the mortgage away to be signed and then brought it back with her signature and my money, it was a done deal. Anyway, she deserved everything he had, and I made sure she got it but I couldn't turn the property over to her until I knew her life was on track and that no one would ever hurt her again. So I built a shrine to her and if anyone were ever to cross her, they would pay the price."

Sebastian sits back down in his chair, swings slightly around so his body is extremely square to Joe's and replies in a serious manner, "Come on, Joe! You're rambling like a madman. If what you're saying is true, it would make no sense in the world to sell the property to Mike Cohen. Honestly, Joe, I told you before, you have given me nothing and I have better things to do than waste my time with your ravings." Sebastian sways his head in disgust and then swings his legs to the side of the chair.

Before he can get to his feet, Joe has a lot more to say, "Don't you go anywhere Cork, you arrogant pig; I haven't finished yet!" Sebastian has both hands on the seat and is ready to push himself up but on hearing the desperation in Joe's voice, he screws his head back in his direction and glares at him out of the corner of his eye. "Two minutes, Joe, and then I will definitely be done, so don't waste anymore of my time."

As Sebastian swings back around to face Joe, Joe glares directly into Sebastian's determined eyes. "Once I bought the place, business began to drop off and even after taking on additional hours at the gym, I still couldn't keep up with my payments, so I made a deal with that mongrel Mike; I told him if he bought the property from me and let me use it, I would buy the old farm back as soon as I can and at double the amount he paid me for it. He agreed and we shook hands on it. No sooner had I sold him the property then Kate tells me she had picked up a huge new chain of stores in the area and she wanted me to do all the deliveries for her. Once I signed the big new contract with Kate, the banks were only too happy to offer me whatever I wanted to borrow but when I went to buy the place back off him, that dirty lanky piece of shit said he wouldn't sell it to me. He told me that a developer had offered him a million dollars for it and that he had put himself in debt to help me out, so he deserved to keep it!"

"Now I will tell you one thing... when I shake hands with someone on a deal it's as good as putting it on paper, so I went away and thought about things; a deal is a deal and I was going to get that property back one way or another. Anyway, a couple of weeks ago I found out his business was going into liquidation, so I approached him at the gym and said I would take over his payments and he could still remain on the deed as half owner. I just couldn't let the place get into someone else's hands but he told me he had already paid the hundred thousand he owed on it and I didn't have a snowflake's chance in hell."

"So I did what I did to any scumbag that runs Kate or me up the wrong way; I took him out to the farm and demanded he tell me where the deed was but he wouldn't and he ended up getting cut down to size like the rest and I know their punishment is nothing in comparison to where they are now!" he says as though he is some sort of necromancer and then continues, "All you have to do is check with my bank and you will see where my loan was paid off. Kate knew nothing about any of it. So if you don't believe me just check it out, Mr Brainless bag of crap.

Joe looks at Sebastian with total contempt and continues, "You can do what you like to me but Kate doesn't deserve to go through hell when she hasn't done what you're saying she's done. I don't care what you think you can do to me because I know that somehow, someday I'll get out and then the two of you will be punished for this travesty of justice. But the books have to be set straight about her so-called father, who was nothing but a scumbag and the lowest animal on the earth," he hisses with indignation.

Joe lets out a small gasp of pleasure and begins relating what he saw as his most brilliant moments. "Kate told me how her father treated her and I knew what that felt like so without telling her I went and confronted him. He pulled a gun on me and told me if I didn't get off his property, I wouldn't be leaving at all. So that evening I rolled up to his farm with a baseball bat; I didn't need a gun to take care of things. I saw a bright light coming from the barn and as I got closer I could see the wall had elevated at the rear and the light was coming up from the cellar below. I sat there for over an hour waiting for him to emerge and when he finally did, wham!"

Sebastian and Paul watch as Joe's eyes light up from the sense of overwhelming power and control he is feeling as he relates his spine-chilling tale. They are also aware of his cold, calculating, demeanour and there is definitely no hiding of guilt, as pride for his heinous deed is mockingly written all over his face. Paul who's catching on fast to Sebastian's objective responds, "That still doesn't prove you killed him; all it proves is you knocked him out."

Joe sways his head from side to side and curls the corner of his top lip. "I wish the two of you would shut the fuck up and let me finish. A few days prior, Kate and I had been discussing a headline in the paper about this guy who had given this woman a date rape drug and I said to her 'how do these guys know how to make this shit?' Kate, being a chemist, couldn't help but tell me how easy the ingredients were to get. So I thought I'd give it a shot – you know just for the fun of it –there are some pesky cats in my neighbourhood that I thought may enjoy a dose or three if you know what I mean.

Anyway, after Kate's old man pulled the gun on me, what better opportunity to test it out? So I dragged his unconscious body into the house, got a funnel and forced the shit down his throat. Then I laid him on the floor near the blinds and made it look like he'd knocked over the oil lamp. Of course, before I set it on fire, I waited long enough for him to regain consciousness and then I sat there as long as I could so I could watch him suffer the way he made Kate suffer. The only thing I regret is, although he was semi-conscious, the drug hadn't worn off enough for him to scream. I would have loved to have heard that," he scoffs at his ludicrous indignity of Kate's father.

Paul looks at him with utter disgust and contempt. "Tell me something else, Joe... what was the point of dressing like Kate?"

Joe's arms are now crossed, his eyes glazed and his nose wrinkles from the sneer on his face. "Seriously? You really are stupid, aren't you? Kate and I are one; she is the kind, gentle side and I'm the strength who takes care of the tough stuff," he jeers in a snake's hiss.

Paul looks at Sebastian curiously as Sebastian signals with his head to leave and Joe is left there with his brow raised and a large grin on his face as if he's in his happy place. Sebastian swings around and pushes to his feet, then looks back down at Joe with a half-cocked smile. "Well, Joe, it looks like you're going away for a long, long time and from what you have told us, you will be doing it alone."

Joe flicks his head back and smirks. "I've been doing it alone most my life, so I'm good with that. Just make sure you watch your back my fat friend; you never know what the future holds for pieces of crap like you!"

Sebastian has already turned to walk away but he stops, glances back over his shoulder and replies, "Whether it's long or short, Sir, it will at least taste of freedom; best of luck to you, my friend." Sebastian smiles confidently, turns and walks out with Paul.

After letting Jim know the outcome of the interviews, they arrange the release of Kate and her sister. Michelle is quickly on her way but on the other side of the coin, Kate says she wants a minute alone to collect herself; so the boys leave her and walk down the corridor to wait outside the interview room for someone to come and pick up Joe and take him to his cell. Paul stands there quiet and withdrawn and Sebastian is concerned.

"What's wrong, Paul? You seem out of sorts."

He looks at Sebastian blankly. "I guess I've just come to the realisation that there's a fine line between someone turning into a serial killer or focusing their anger toward a better life. Tell me something, Seb... what makes a hideous creature like Joe do the things he's done? You know, there were times in my life where others would say offensive things to me and when I had had enough I would walk away and there have been other times where I have felt so angry, it wouldn't have been hard for me to wrap my hands around their necks and throttle them; So why not me?"

Sebastian can see this case has aroused something in Paul that's been suppressed and is now surfacing as unfinished business, so he tries to explain, "Apart from all the events from childhood and onward that occur in a person's life, genetics can also have a bearing on the emotional tolerance one exhibits. Take Joe for instance; something snapped inside him like a weak limb and it sent him hurtling head first into a world that only he could understand. I had an idea that Joe was our culprit when I interviewed people from his old neighbourhood. Even in his childhood, he presented with narcissist and psychotic traits. In his case, we have both childhood events and genetic traits at play. His father was a cold heartless human being with narcissistic traits and on top of that he treated both Joe and his mother cruelly. The worst thing of all was, unlike Kate, there was no escape for him at school either, as he was constantly bullied by bigger children about his size. Eventually the bullying roles became reversed into a psychotic perversion of reality. There was never a lot of hope for him to rise above it all."

"Then when we look at Kate's life, even I find it hard to believe she hasn't inherited the negative and cruel traits of her father but there are sometimes exceptions to the rules. Perhaps the difference in your and her life may be as simple as you both had solid grounding and boundaries; in your case, your mother provided you with love and encouragement and her adopted parents may have done the same for her."

Paul's brow creases and he looks directly into Sebastian's eyes, as a son would to his father, and says, "I can see now why you were the best of the best when it came to psychology."

Sebastian smiles with returned admiration and replies, "What do you mean 'were'?"

Paul grins, turns to walk away but Sebastian is quick to stop him. "No, seriously, Paul, what do you mean 'were'?" Just as Paul is about to answer, Joe emerges from the interview room handcuffed and escorted by a burly policeman. He sneers with a curled upper lip at Paul as he is about to start his trip up the corridor toward the holding cells. Coincidently Kate turns the corner and proceeds down the corridor toward them on her way out and Joe's delighted eyes follow her every move as she works her way toward him. It's not long before she crosses Joe's path on the way through and he smiles at her affectionately and she smiles back at him as though she is in friendly company but then puts her head down as she passes Sebastian and Paul.

Sebastian's brow folds as a sense of indifference starts stealing over him. He curiously looks back at Paul. "Did you see that?" he says and then casts a glance back down the corridor toward her.

Paul, still lamenting and staring at Kate's back as she disappears around the corner out of sight, turns his head slowly to face Sebastian. "See what, Seb?"

"Kate's smile just then! Surely you saw it?"

Paul squints as though Sebastian has lost his marbles. "She has known him for a long time, Seb. It could have been just a nervous grin or one of affection for a sick friend. I don't know! Anyway, what difference does it make?"

Sebastian gives a little flick of his shoulders and head and responds to Paul's reply, "Yes, I guess that's true but given the same circumstances wouldn't you show anger, fear or even avoidance towards Joe, knowing what he has put you through or what he has done? It just seems to me that an affectionate smile is oddly strange under the circumstances. But perhaps you're right... people do react in peculiar ways under peculiar circumstances."

Paul grins thoughtfully. "Well, he has confessed to the murders and he has given us a detailed account of how it all went down, so we do know there's no doubt that he was there when the murders occurred. Now, can I buy you a coffee, Seb?"

Sebastian smiles as he puts his hand on Paul's shoulder. "Of course you can. Let's go! I know just the place."

Sebastian finishes his paperwork and makes his way to Jim's office where he finds Emily on the phone. He places his file on her desk, points to it and then to Jim's office door but as he is about to turn and leave, Emily's expression becomes serious and her eyebrows meet while she frantically waves her head from side to side making her slender cheeks wobble. Then she holds up the palm of her free hand and Sebastian sits down and waits until she is off the phone. "Sorry, Seb, but before you go, Jim said he needed to speak to you," she swings her swivel chair and rises from it, all in one motion. Emily knocks on Jim's door and pokes her head in his office. "Seb's here to see you, Jim."

An immediate reply comes enthusiastically back, "Good, good! Send him straight in thanks, Emily!" Before she can say a word, Sebastian is right behind her, ready to enter.

Jim's sitting forward in his seat signing off on a document as Sebastian makes his way to the chair in front of his desk. He looks up, happily drops the pen and places the papers to the side. "Paul has given me a brief indication on the interviews and Joe's confession and I just wanted to thank you personally as this has taken an enormous load off my shoulders but you already know that, don't you?" Sebastian smiles, nods in the affirmative and Jim continues, "Anyway, I have already expressed my appreciation to Paul by telling him he has been promoted off the rookie list. I suggested to Paul that we would like him to partner up with another detective, so we could spread you across other teams."

Sebastian's eyebrows close in. "I'm a bit put out by this, Jim. I'm a man of routine and I'm not sure I would like to be moved around from one team to another, so I may have to reconsider my position here, especially if this is the way you thank someone for their good work." Sebastian replies uncompromisingly and is about to stand when Jim throws his open palms forward. "Whoa! Hang on a minute before you go jumping the gun, Seb!" Sebastian eases back into his chair and Jim continues, "Anyway, Paul pulled pretty much the same expression on his face as you did and told me that he would prefer to work with you but understood if you would prefer to move on, he would accept your decision. After my conversation with Paul, I spoke to the

Commissioner and he believes that the two of you could benefit other teams from time to time but only if you were to agree to this offer."

Sebastian looks down at his cane and smiles then pushes his chin up. "So the young fellow wants to stay with the old boy, does he?"

Jim smiles. "So it seems"

Sebastian pulls down a more serious veil over his face. "Well, I really don't see the need for me to change a team that is working well together, but before making a decision on the other matter of working with different groups together, I feel it would be unfair to do so without discussing this with my partner first."

Jim relaxes back into his chair. "I'm so glad to hear that, Seb. I wouldn't want it any other way. There's just one more thing that you may be able to enlighten me on. When we went through Mike Cohen's house looking for clues, we came across a locker key so I asked an officer to drop into the gym and bring back the contents but the only thing he found in there was this," he leans forward and pulls a document from his drawer and slides it over to Sebastian and as Sebastian begins unfolding it, Jim continues, "Its a deed to the farm where the murders were committed. Did you know that Steve Cohen owns that property?"

Sebastian looks at the deed and without looking back up replies, "Yes, yes, I did."

Jim slumps back into his chair. "Okay... didn't this ever strike you to be important information that I should know about?"

Sebastian ignores his question, looks back up from the now unfolded paper and deep into Jim's eyes. "I'm wondering if I can call on that debt that you said you owed me and ask you to forget you ever saw this document. If you will allow me, I will give it back to its rightful owner."

"I would need an explanation and a lot of convincing to turn it over, so tell me what this is about and I will do my best."

Sebastian explains about the property and how Steve's son had used the money that his father had loaned him to buy it; he also went on to explain that the money for the land would be enough to pay off Mike's debt and put his parents back on their feet. He continued to tell Jim that if the creditors found out, they may claim the property, so they can't know that the hundred thousand for the property was taken from Mike's business account.

Jim scratches his head and thinks for a silent moment. "Sorry, Seb. I'm not sure if I heard you correctly; did you say that Mike's father asked you to bring this deed in to show me because Kate was a suspect and he wanted us to know that she had once owned the property where Mike was killed? Look, tell him I said thanks very much but we have proof Kate didn't do it and we already have enough evidence on Joe to send him away for the rest of his life. Oh and before you go, do me a favour please and make sure that deed gets back to him safely, won't you, Seb?"

Sebastian's cheeks light up with a smile. "Most definitely, Jim. I will drop it off on my way home."

Jim smiles back. "So are we even now, Seb?"

Sebastian rises to his feet. "More than even, my friend. Thanks again!" Sebastian reaches across the desk and shakes Jim's hand in gratitude and then heads out of his office in the direction of the parking bay.

On arrival he gets in his car and makes a quick phone call to ensure the Cohens are in so he can make a detour on his way home. A short conversation ensues and once off the phone he makes his way through some fairly heavy traffic to their house. Any other time Sebastian may have felt worn and irritable after such a big day and then having to spend half an hour in the midst of honking horns and exhaust fumes, but on arrival at the Cohen's house he alights from the car in a spritely manner, works his way up their pathway to the veranda at pace and taps on the door.

Sebastian's overly positive mood rapidly develops a new perspective when Steve Cohen answers the door like a man who is only breathing because it is instinctive to do so. Sebastian warmly shakes his limp hand and Steve escorts him into the lounge. "Mary is upstairs, lying down, and I would rather let her be at the moment. We asked the bank if we could have some grace on our loan as I can't go to work and leave her the way she is but they told me if I can't make the payments they would have to foreclose." Mr Cohen's voice begins to break and he takes some long, slow breaths before he begins again, "Sorry, I shouldn't be burdening you with my problems. Believe it or not, I used to talk to Michael when I had things on my mind; I really miss that." Mr Cohen's sad eyes drift slowly down, then he takes a deep short broken breath and exhales as if blowing out candles. "Sorry again, Sebastian. Can I get you a coffee or tea?

Sebastian smiles with gratification. "No I'm fine, thank you. I can't stay long but there are a couple of important matters I must speak to you about. The first is we have charged a man with your son's murder." Mr Cohen's lip begins to quiver and Sebastian can see he is having trouble responding, so he leaves the sofa, squats down next to the arm of Mr Cohen's chair and places his hand on his shoulder. "It's okay, there's only you and I here. You can let it out now."

Steve Cohen throws his open hands over his face and sobs uncontrollably into them. Sebastian pats his shoulder until he eventually runs out of tears and then he moves graciously back to the sofa and waits patiently for him to find some composure.

"I'm so sorry, Sebastian. I think everything has finally caught up with me," he leans forward and takes several tissues from a box sitting on the coffee table, blows his nose and continues, "Was it anyone we know?"

Sebastian waves his head in the negative and responds. "No, but it was someone Michael knew at the gym."

Mr Cohen looks at Sebastian inquisitively through polished eyes. "Why? What would make him kill my son?"

Sebastian reaches his hand into the inside pocket of his jacket and holds out the deed. "This. This is why." Mr Cohen accepts the document and begins unfolding it as Sebastian tells him its history.

"Once he found out what the property was really worth he borrowed the money off you to secure it. His business was already in the hands of the receivers and too late to save but he wanted to make sure your debt was well and truly taken care of. I have contacted the company that wants the land and they will be in touch with you tomorrow with an offer well over one million dollars. Hopefully, it will not only pay off the debt you have been left with but you will also be able to retire comfortably. There is one favour I must ask you though and I wouldn't ask if it wasn't considerably important: if anyone should ask you about the property it is imperative you tell them that you bought it, not your son. I know I am asking a lot of you but I need your word on this, please; otherwise, everything your son did for you will be lost. You may want to look at this as his legacy."

Mr Cohen looks into Sebastian's eyes and says, "You have my word. I don't know how to thank you, Sebastian, but I do know that this will help towards my wife's recovery. It was hard enough to lose our son and then we had no idea what we would do if they took our family home; he was born in this house, you know. I will make sure his name is clear of any debt and I will also put some aside for a scholarship in his name to help up and coming tri-athletes."

Sebastian stands, shakes Mr Cohen's hand and begins his journey home.

Over the following days, time passes agonisingly slow for Sebastian and he is finding his world so incredibly monotonous that even the ticking of the antique mantle clock that has so often soothed his tensions while having a quiet drink and read in the study, is getting under his skin; so he decides he needs a project and begins spending an unusual amount of time locked away in his office at the rear of the house. Cynthia doesn't object to a certain amount of 'me time' but normally when Sebastian is home, he often requires her help for one thing or another and even though it can become a source of annoyance, she misses it when it doesn't happen, so she decides to knock on his door. After entering she can see a wad of papers sitting on his desk and he's at the fax machine with his back to her, methodically scanning over one newly printed document, while blindly tearing off yet another.

"Sorry for disturbing you, Seb, but I have been feeling a little concerned for you. Are you okay?"

He turns and looks back over his shoulder at her. "Of course, my love; why do you ask?"

Cynthia gracefully glides over to him and puts her arms over his shoulders. "Well the only chance I get to see you lately is at meal times and I thought now that the case you were working on is officially over, we could spend a little more time together."

He responds affectionately, "I'm sorry, Cynthia. I took on a little project of my own because I thought too much of me would get under your skin."

Cynthia exhales a deep sigh. "Too much of anyone gets under my skin, darling, but not enough of you can be like losing a piece of me. Anyway, what is this project you are working on?"

He kisses her on the forehead and busily ambles to the rear of his desk, places his new arrival on top of the other papers and then stoops over to open the top drawer. "Never mind that; I have a little surprise for you. Remember that play that was showing at the beachside theatre? You know the one that all your friends were raving about?"

Cynthia smirks. "You mean the one you said wild dogs couldn't drag you to?"

Sebastian eyes look up from his stooped position. "Yes, that's the one."

"The one you said you would rather spend your time learning to crochet than attend some unknown amateurish production of that sort?"

Sebastian now upright tilts his head slightly to one side. "Okay, I get the point; I was a little over the top with my criticism. Anyway, I also realised we haven't been doing much together of late, so I thought we could kill two birds with one stone. This Friday I have booked the two of us for lunch at one of my favourite little restaurants near the theatre and here is a printout of the tickets for the play." Sebastian smiles and holds out the tickets as though he is presenting a trophy to a well deserving recipient.

Cynthia stands there with her head pushed forward and mouth agape then responds, "Really?"

He smiles lovingly. "Of course! Would I lie to you?" Cynthia frowns for a second and Sebastian is quick to pick up on it.

"What? What's wrong, my love?"

She closes her eyes and releases a deep sigh. "We have Paul and his fiancée coming for dinner on Saturday and there is so much to do before they come. I was really counting on getting it done on Friday."

"What if I help you Saturday morning?"

Her head shoots up again. "Would you? Could you?"

"Of course! All you have to do is let me know what you want and I will do it."

Friday arrives, the weather is windy and cold and Sebastian tells Cynthia to wait inside until he reverses the Bentley from the garage but she is without patience and keen to get going, so she waits rigidly on the porch with her gloved hands hidden deep inside the pockets of her woollen red coat.

When the car eventually pulls up alongside the house, she quickly hops in, closes the door and wiggles out of her coat. Sebastian looks at her curiously and she gives him a questioning glare back. "Well? It was too cold to take it off out there!"

He waves his head rapidly from side to side. "If you had waited inside like I asked you to, there wouldn't have been a need to put yourself through such contortions in the first place!"

She folds her coat neatly and twists herself into a position to put her knees on the front seat and places her coat in the back while Sebastian sits quietly glaring straight in front of him waiting for Cynthia to complete her task so he can get underway. Cynthia swings herself halfway back around, caresses his hair, kisses Sebastian on the cheek and then buckles up. "Well, what are we waiting for?"She says with a cheeky grin on her face.

Sebastian looks sideways at her, then back again and mumbles, "Driving Miss crazy!"Cynthia smiles, Sebastian motors forward and within minutes they are headed out of their large black gates and making a run through the smog and haze of the bustling city traffic. Once out of town they relax into the drive while cutting through the centre of patchwork quilted amber to green paddocks lined with white railed fences until they eventually reach a road that winds its way in and out of sight of the choppy blue ocean. The wind outside the car whistles intermittently as it flows over the chrome mirrors on each guard and the odd whooshing gust is so strong it even sways the solid old Bentley on straight stretches where flat paddocks exist.

Cynthia loves the ocean and begins craving for more as she gazes out of the passenger window toward its vast beauty at every opportunity she can get. Her childlike happiness picks up further as they cross over a bridge that spans an inlet lined by green grassy knolls where flocks of pelicans gather along the flat white bordering sands and protruding grey timber jetties, as they shelter from the prevailing robust winds and rollercoaster swells. Cynthia swings her head back toward Sebastian with thoughtful eyes. "We really should have brought the camera, Seb. Look at that scenery."

But Sebastian doesn't answer; he just glances across and contently smiles and then refocuses on the road. A moment later Sebastian hears a strange loud noise like a passing car and he is soon inhaling the recognisable odour of kelp and salty air as it comes bursting through Cynthia's wound down window with a gush. "WHATTHEHECKAREYOUDOING, WOMAN? DO YOU WANT US BOTH TO CATCH OUR DEATH?"

Cynthia's long, glowing, ebony hair sweeps and swirls around her face in gay abandon as it blows about in the roaring wind. She turns laughingly with a shout, "NO, SEB, I WANT US BOTH TO LIVE!"

Sebastian, trying to steer the wheel with one hand while brushing his thick salt and pepper hair down with the other, sees her snatching at the strands caught in her mouth and across her face and tightens his lips as he holds back his own merriment with great difficulty. "CYNTHIA, MY LOVE... I'M BLOODYWELL FREEZING!

She winds up the window and then looks back at him half jokingly and half scornfully. "Old Fuddy-Duddy!"

He glances back at her with messed up hair and red cheeks and they both burst into laughter; they continue their merriment for the rest of the journey and it's not long before they turn up a narrow paved road, lined with hedges until it opens into a large parking area surrounded by pine log railings. Sebastian pulls the Bentley up as close as possible to the old building, which was once a lighthouse but has since been skilfully renovated into an elite restaurant, sitting high on a cliff with a sheer drop to the ocean below. They quickly snatch up their coats from the back seat and half run, half walk as they clumsily try to put them on in the strong winds, while working their way toward the reception area and inner warmth of the restaurant. The gales are cold, fierce and relentless and the conifers that normally stand tall and firm are swaying like hula dancers in the howling gusts.

Once inside, Sebastian and Cynthia follow one of the staff to a cosy secluded table for two with floor to ceiling windows that overlook the ocean and they sit there quietly gazing out at the undulating and surging white capped waves that are being whisked into a frenzy by the gale force winds. Even the seagulls which would normally fly with rhythm and style find themselves soaring and diving in an out of control manner as they follow the last of the fishing boats into the harbour.

Cynthia, who seems momentarily caught in a hypnotic trance, ponderously brings her thoughts back to the room and romantically gazes at her husband. "It seems ironic that one can feel so warm, calm and safe while gazing out over the exact opposite, don't you think, Seb?"

He grins at her amorously. "Most definitely, my love. The Ying and the Yang are total opposites yet create a perfect balance. A bit like us in some ways, don't you think?"

She reaches over the table and puts both her hands on the top of his. "There are times when you can be so romantic, Seb! Thank you for bringing me, darling."

"You're welcome. Now, what has happened to those bloody menus? I'm famished," he says seriously, making Cynthia's eyes leap in the direction of the ceiling. The waitress soon appears to take their orders. After lunch they drive down the road to the theatre and Sebastian goes up to the ticket box to get their passes; then returns back and hands Cynthia her pass. "There you are, my love. Would you mind going in ahead of me? Something I ate at the restaurant doesn't seem to be agreeing with my stomach."

She looks at him with concern. "Would you rather we went home, Seb? Or perhaps we should go to the clinic?"

He smiles at her calmingly. "No, no, I'm fine; nothing more than a tummy ache, that's all. You go ahead. I'll join you presently, my love."

It's getting close to interval and Cynthia has been so enchanted by the play, she doesn't realise Sebastian has been missing for almost an hour but when she does she begins to panic until he comes strolling down the aisle with an armful of snacks. "Are you okay, Seb? I was getting worried," she whispers.

Sebastian takes a seat next to her and whispers back, "I am now, my love, thank you. Here, I brought you a cold drink" She smiles at him, accepts his offerings and they enjoy the rest of the play together and then head home. That evening Cynthia tells Sebastian how much she has appreciated the wonderful day she has had and they retire to an early evening.

It's Saturday morning and the alarm goes off on Cynthia's side of the bed and she flings back the blankets not only on her side but on Sebastian's as well.

Sebastian, still half asleep, remains in a foetal position while reaching down to his shins in an effort to find the comforting covers that have been removed. "Cynthia! What's going on?" he asks while rubbing the tips of his fingers up and down each side of his brow.

"Come on, Seb! We have a million things to do today. Don't you remember? Paul and his fiancée are coming to dinner this evening and I need to get to the supermarket to buy some fresh fillets of fish and something scrumptious for dessert."

Sebastian, now sitting upright, muffles a yawn into the back of his hand and while peering at her from baggy eyes he responds, "What's that got to do with me?"

Cynthia glides over to the bed, thrusts her hands on her hips and with lips pulled tight she lets him have it, "Sebastian Cork, have you forgotten already? You promised me you would help today; otherwise I would have stayed home yesterday and had everything ready for our guests! All I am asking you to do today is prepare the vegetables so there is less for me to worry about when I get back from shopping; now I don't think that is asking too much, **do you**?"

Sebastian can see the look in his wife's eyes is not one to be contended with, "No, no not at all. It slipped my mind temporarily. Just give me a moment to collect myself and I will head downstairs for a shower."

Cynthia, still in a hurry to get ready, turns around in the direction of the bathroom but not before giving him a grateful glance. "I'll leave a note on the kitchen table of what needs doing to make it easier for you. Sebastian huffs, swings out of bed and begins his journey to the shower downstairs. Once they are both ready they join each other in the kitchen for breakfast, Cynthia gives Sebastian a list of what she needs from him and then leaves to buy the required groceries.

The morning wears on slowly until Cynthia eventually arrives home from shopping and finds Sebastian sitting at the kitchen table reading the local paper and sipping on coffee. He looks over his shoulder as she enters the room and holds his mug in the air. "Can I get you a coffee, my love?" he says nonchalantly.

"Seb! You were supposed to have prepared the vegetables for me! Please, please, please don't tell me you have forgotten!" she says desperately as her arms go limp with shopping bags.

He swings around in his chair. "In the oven my love, just waiting for you to turn them on."

Cynthia places the bags of groceries on the floor and throws her arms around his neck. "I'm sorry, Seb. I was just concerned that you may have forgotten. You do have a habit of doing that sort of thing, you know."

He kisses her and whispers. "Only when my mind is preoccupied with other things; I am sure you will get the opportunity to rouse me up again when a new case comes along."

She straightens back up and smacks him on the shoulder. "You make me sound like I am at you consistently!"

He laughs out loud. "Not at all, my love! It's never consistent; otherwise I would be expecting it."

Cynthia hits him again. "Enough of this frivolity; I have too much to do!" So she begins unpacking her grocery bags and he buries his head back into his paper while sipping on his coffee.

The afternoon flies by and it's not long until Paul and his fiancée, Chelsea, are due to arrive. Cynthia has showered, dressed and worked diligently on her makeup and when Sebastian makes his way back upstairs and into the bedroom, she does a little pirouette and asks him how she looks.

He looks her up and down and responds with, "You are a picture of sartorial elegance, my love."

She smiles lovingly at him and before she has a chance to return the compliment the doorbell chimes and Cynthia makes her graceful unhurried way downstairs toward the front door, while Sebastian follows her down to the landing but then splits off in another direction. Cynthia welcomes Paul and introduces herself to his fiancée with an eloquent smile and a peck on the cheek then points them to the hat and coat stand in the hall. She then leads them into the den where Sebastian is waiting and he approaches Paul, shakes his hand and then moves towards Paul's fiancée.

"Hello, you must be Chelsea. Paul has told me so much about you," he says and then greets her with a kiss on the cheek. She's a tall slender girl with large blue eyes and short dark hair and he doesn't have to bend to kiss her like he does with Cynthia.

She smiles graciously at her host and replies, "I hope he only told you good things!"

Sebastian smiles back. "Of course, of course. Now, can I get the two of you a drink?"

Sebastian gets Paul a beer and Chelsea a mineral water and while Sebastian and Paul are talking, Cynthia breaks the ice with Chelsea. "I hear you are a model Chelsea; are you freelance or contracted?"

"A bit of both, Cynthia. My parents have a line of lingerie stores and I also do work for my aunt. You might have heard of her... Estelle Hollingsworth?"

A surprised look brushes over Cynthia's face. "Of course I have! And not only is she famous but she is a lovely person as well. My friend Clarissa and I run the odd charity event from time to time and your aunt has been kind enough to be a guest and she has also sent us some of her new season labels to auction off."

Chelsea tells her she probably modelled at those fundraisers and Cynthia says she thought she had seen her somewhere before.

Meanwhile, Sebastian explains to Paul that Jim had also approached him about breaking up the partnership and he wasn't prepared to work with anyone else, so they will be staying together. He also explains that he told Jim he wouldn't make a decision about working with other teams until he had spoken to Paul about it. "So what do you think Paul?" A huge smile appears on Paul's face and a concerned look grows on Sebastian's face. "What's so amusing, Paul?"

"Think about it, Seb! You have enough problems working with me. How the heck would you be able to cope with others who probably have a lot less patience than I do?"

Sebastian glares silently at him and is about to respond when Cynthia comes over and intervenes, "Sorry, boys. It's time we moved to the dining area. Dinner should be ready by now."

Sebastian squints at Paul. "I wouldn't mind finishing this conversation at a more convenient time, Paul; that is; if you feel I am capable of coping with it?"

Paul smiles again. "Definitely, Seb! You know me; I cope with most of your issues."

Sebastian takes a deep breath and is about to snap at Paul's statement when Cynthia grabs him by the arm. "Come on, boys! Dinner will soon be cold if we don't move along."

Chelsea helps Cynthia bring the food to the table and they sit down to eat. While Cynthia is passing the potatoes to Paul, she enquires about his health.

"I'm good now, Cynthia. Most the effects wore off overnight. Thanks for asking."

She looks down the table to her husband and then back to Paul. "I felt obligated to, Paul; after all, it was my husband that put your life in danger in the first place."

Sebastian puts his knife and fork on his plate with a clang and begins wiping his mouth with his napkin. "It wasn't like that, Cynthia. I had no idea who the next victim would be!"

Cynthia glares back down the table at him. "Well, you should have at least known where your partner was at the time!"

Paul interjects, "I'm sorry to interrupt, Cynthia, but I really do have to take the blame for Seb not knowing where I was; I had forgotten to charge the battery on my phone and when I charged it overnight at the hospital, there were numerous missed calls from Seb."

Sebastian looks at Paul with admiration and then up the table to Cynthia. "I tried to explain that to you, Cynthia. I only knew where the next murder was going to happen, not who the victim would be. Anyway, Paul was never in danger. He is a fit young man and we had medics on hand just in case. Not only that, we knew the drug that was being used and what we would need to negate it."

Paul attempts to change the subject before it gets tense. "It really is a shame what Kate had been put through, don't you agree, Seb?"

Sebastian takes a sip of water and surprises Paul with his statement. "I'm not sure about that, Paul. As I have explained before, not everything is always what it seems."

Paul looks up from his plate. "You're not still on about that look she gave Joe, are you?"

"That's only part of it, Paul. After we finished our investigation that look kept playing on my mind and as I had some spare time, I thought I might delve further into Kate's childhood and curiously enough, I found there were reports of Kate's adopted father abusing her as a child and the school had insisted she see a psychologist due to her inability to connect or communicate with other children. The psychologist's report was interesting reading; she was still wetting her bed at the age of twelve and had a lack of connection to any living thing."

"The other interesting fact was her adopted father would take Kate away rock fishing whenever they had a long weekend and the two of them would stay in a shack near the beach that one of his friends owned but her adopted mother didn't like fishing so she wouldn't go. I phoned an old friend of the family and she told me Kate would plead with her mother to stay home with her but her mother thought it would be good for Kate to spend some bonding time with him."

Paul, with his head tilted to one side, looks at Sebastian inquisitively. "She was a little girl, Seb, and a lot of little girls don't like fishing. That doesn't prove anything."

Sebastian swallows a piece of fish and continues his explanation, "You are right about that, Paul but on their last fishing trip, her adopted father never returned. Apparently he couldn't swim and even though he had fished this spot since he was a young boy, the coroner's report said a freak wave had washed him in and he had drowned. There were no witnesses except for Kate and it was reported that she had called for help but it was too late by the time someone arrived."

Paul, seemingly confused says, "Okay but that doesn't prove anything except that it was a freak accident."

Sebastian, now frustrated as he seemingly doesn't want to get into a full explanation, looks over at Cynthia and then back to Paul. "I decided to take a drive to the spot where he had died and found an isolated ledge which was approximately five feet up from a section of deep water and fully protected by other ledges on either side so the freak wave could have only hit him face on."

Paul interrupts, "Yes, but it is still possible that he could have been dragged in by the backwash, isn't it?"

"It is possible but not probable, Paul."

"Why is that?"

Sebastian continues, "They actually retrieved his body from the water and, of course, there had to be an inquest into his death even though it all seemed straight forward; the coroner's report read that the only marks found on his body was one circular bruise toward the centre of his shoulder blades and abrasions to the skin of his fingers from desperately trying to hang onto the rocks and work his way out of the water."

Cynthia chips in, "That seems feasible; he probably hit his back when he was washed over by the wave."

Sebastian nods in the affirmative. "Yes that is a valid point and I would normally agree to this if I hadn't been out there myself but this is a flat shelf with no protruding round rocks. If it did happen that way..."

Cynthia interrupts again, "There would have been either no bruising or a lot of bruising to his back."

Sebastian smiles. "Exactly, my love. And the other thing is, there was no bruising to the back of his head either. The only plausible explanation I could come up with is he was shoved from behind by something similar in shape to a baseball bat. As fascinating as all this is, it is only speculation and perhaps we should give Kate the benefit of the doubt, so let's forget about that for now and enjoy this wonderful meal." Paul has listened with intent and at first he was incredulous but he has worked with Sebastian long enough now to understand that he rarely bases his deductions on emotional persuasions but more on facts and probabilities.

At the other end of the room, Cynthia puts both her hands on the table and pushes back into her chair. "Wait just one minute, Sebastian Cork! The only opportunity you have had to be near a beach since finalising this case was when you asked me to go with you because we hadn't had much time together. So that's what took you so long when you left me in the theatre?"

Sebastian, knowing he has disgraced himself again, tips his head forward and his eyes move from one side and then to the other.

"Sebastian, I asked you a question!"

Sebastian's eyes rise to meet Cynthia's. "Actually, you made a statement my love, but this probably isn't the time or place to discuss the matter. Wow! Look how fresh that asparagus is; did you get that from the grocers down the road?" he declares nervously.

Cynthia throws her eyes toward the ceiling but realises, if she pursues the matter it will make their guests feel uncomfortable, but still has problems putting a rein on her sarcasm. "Yes, Sebastian, the same one where we always shop. Oh and, by the way, we will finish our discussion on our little trip to the seaside at a later date. Now, Paul and Chelsea, is there anything else I can get you?"

Paul smiles and looks at Chelsea amorously and she smiles and gazes back into his eyes. "No thanks, Cynthia, but there is something Chelsea and I would like to ask you and Seb," he says, looking from Cynthia and then to Sebastian.

"Of course. Go ahead!" Cynthia replies while smiling curiously.

"Well, as you know, Chelsea and I are engaged and we are hoping to marry on the first Sunday of summer and we would love you both to be there."

Cynthia rises from her seat and holds her arms out to Paul and he meets her with a hug. "We would love to be there, wouldn't we, Seb?" she says as she looks back over her shoulder at her husband.

Sebastian has also risen from his seat and is almost with Paul and Cynthia when he replies, "Of course, of course, we will be there with bells on!" Cynthia moves to hug Chelsea and Sebastian shakes Paul's hand but gets a shock when he is pulled in close to Paul and hugged warmly. Sebastian's eyes move rapidly from side to side and then relax as a fatherly grin draws across his face. The rest of the evening goes brilliantly.